He Loves Me, He Loves You Not 5

Remi's World

A Novel

MYCHEA

Good2Go Publishing

ISBN:

Copyright ©2015 by Mychea

Published 2015 by Good2Go Publishing

7311 W. Glass Lane • Laveen, AZ 85339

www.good2gopublishing.com

twitter @good2gobooks

G2G@good2gopublishing.com

Facebook.com/good2gopublishing

ThirdLane Marketing: Brian James

Brian@good2gopublishing.com

Cover design: Davida Baldwin

<u>Books by This Author</u>

Coveted

Vengeance

He Loves Me, He Loves You Not

He Loves Me, He Loves You Not 2

He Loves Me, He Loves You Not 3

He Loves Me, He Loves You Not 4

He Loves Me, He Loves You Not 5

My Boyfriend's Wife

My Boyfriend's Wife 2 (Coming Soon)

U Promised (ebook short)

<u>*DVD*</u>

Stage Play of My Boyfriend's Wife

Acknowledgments

Novel #8! Can you believe it!?! I cannot. This has been such an amazing journey, one that I definitely could never have made without all of you, my amazing readers. You mean the world to me. I truly hope that you enjoy the last installment of the He Loves Me, He Loves You Not series! But please don't worry I have many more exciting books coming your way.

Special thanks to my street/virtual team Leandra Baker, Candace Wallace and

Email: mychea@mychea.com

Website: www.mychea.com

He Loves Me,
He Loves You Not 5

Remi's World

RECAP

HE LOVES ME
HE LOVES YOU NOT 4

Harris was enjoying the dad life. His son Jaxon was his whole world. Only two months old, and Jaxon was already holding his head up, smiling, and responding to his dad's voice. "I love you little guy."

"Aww, what's going on in here?"

Harris smiled at the sound of Payton's voice. Payton was his girlfriend and she had been the godsend he needed after his momentary lapse of judgment with Avionne. Payton was a nurse at Anne Arundel Medical Center where Jaxon was born. She'd been present the day his buddies had taken Avionne into custody and had felt compassion for Harris. Payton had stepped right in to fill the void of Jaxon being motherless.

"Someone enjoying Papa time?" Payton asked.

"You know it. I can't get enough if this little guy."

"And he obviously can't get enough of you either," she laughed.

"That's a great thing," Harris responded, as Jaxon yawned in his arms.

"I'm going to put this sleepy punkin' down for a nap before I head out on my trip."

"Okay," Harris said, handing Jaxon to Payton, loathe about letting his son go for even a second, but understanding that naptime was a valuable part of his day. Babies are so addictive. *Who would have thought that I would actually love this whole parenting thing?*

Retrieving the mail from the kitchen counter, he noticed a letter from Avionne. He had to give her credit that she was one persistent woman. He received a letter every day that the mail ran, six days a week from her. He typically tossed them into the trash, but his curiosity was getting the best of him. What is it that she possibly had to say every day of the week?

Harris,

I know that we have our differences and you feel as if I'm undeserving of your time, but can you please send me a photo of our son? Please put yourself in my shoes for one second. I haven't seen my baby boy since he was four days old and was ripped away from me. Please Harris, just one photo. I'm begging you and I've never begged anyone for anything. I'm his mother. I can survive where I am if I just have something to hold on to. Please allow me the opportunity to see his face. Do you realize that I have no idea how my baby boy looks? None whatsoever. I know someone in there that you have a heart. Maybe a misplaced sense of trust, but a good heart nevertheless. At least consider it.

Xoxoxoxoxo,

Avi

Harris lay her letter on the table as he gave her request some thought. In all honesty, what would it hurt to let a mother see a photo of the child that she had birthed? It's not as if she was going to get a chance to hold him, her name wasn't even on the birth certificate, so there really was no way for her to stake claim over Jaxon.

I can oblige her and send one photo, he thought. *Yeah that's what I'll do. What can a photo hurt?*

***

"What you in for?" a heavy southern accent questioned her.

Ignoring the tall, freckle-faced red head, Avionne wasn't in the mood to make conversation with anyone. The police in Maryland had extradited her back to North Carolina to let their police force handle the murder case they had against her for Kamilah. A case that her baby daddy, Harris, was going to testify in. *I so disappointed in myself. They caught me slipping. It won't happen again.*

"When someone speaks to you, it's impolite to not respond," the red head continued, beginning to irk Avionne's nerves.

"Murder," Avionne's cold hard stare met the surprised one of the red head. *Exactly bitch. Back up off me.* "Any other questions?"

Her inquisitive fellow inmate became moot after that and walked away. *Good. Teach you to be in others people business. I never, not one time, asked what got anyone else put in here because I don't care.* Hair braided straight back like Queen Latifah's in the movie *Set It Off*, no make-up, an orange jump suit, white socks, and Nike slides, Avionne felt as if she had never been the worse for wear. Rapidly losing weight because she refused to eat any of the food provided to her for fear of food poisoning.

After dinner, Avionne was glad to be back in her cell. She needed to concentrate on a plan to get out of this place and make her way back to Maryland so that she could see her son. Picking up the photo that Harris had sent her in the mail, her heart melted every time she gazed at her baby boy. She was grateful that Harris had finally deemed it necessary for her to see what her baby looked like. She had begged him enough in all of the letters that she had written him.

She found it amazing how much that her priorities had changed with the birth of her baby. She wanted to be with her son all the time. She would have been able to handle this place if it weren't for that, but with her seed being out in the world without her, she needed to be with him. He was a part of her and she craved the sight of him. While in the hospital she'd called him Lucas, but she knew for a fact that Harris had named him Jaxon Harris Smith, but she didn't care. He would always be Lucas to her. The losers in Maryland hadn't even allowed her time to sign her baby's birth certificate. *Bastards.*

Sitting on the bunk, she pulled her sketch of the Sheriff's Prison Farm out from under her mattress. While living in Greensboro, she'd studied and converted to memory the blueprints of each facility in the event that she was ever caught for any of her fun escapades that she enjoyed partaking in. In her spare time, she had previously tunneled through the entire prison center so that she could have an escape route. Her only question was when she would have an opportunity to pull off this illustrious stunt.

"Avionne, you have a visitor."

Great.

After finishing with her security check, Avionne checked in at the visitor's desk and smiled when she saw her guest waiting for her.

"Get up and give me a hug, Chica!"

Her visitor laughed as she stood, "Same crazy Avi I see."

"Payton, girl, it has been a long time," she said as they sat down. "How are things out in Maryland?"

"Girl, your baby is the most adorable little sumo wrestler in the world."

"Oh, I bet he is. Even though I don't think little and sumo wrestler belong in the same sentence," Avionne laughed. "I'm so jealous you get to see him every day. Thank you so much for halting your life for me."

"It is never a problem, ever. What else are cousins supposed to do if they don't help one another out? Family over everything, honey. Plus your baby daddy is one fine piece of work. I don't mind sopping him up with good loving every night." Payton laughed.

"Gross, "Avionne frowned her face up. "Please spare me the details. I know what it's like and you need to remember not to get too attached to him. He's a dead man walking."

"I know, I know. I'm just helping to make his last days a little more pleasant."

Avionne burst into laughter. "Payton you are good and crazy, you know that?"

"So I've been told." She leaned in across the table and spoke lowly, "So, what's the plan? When we getting you out of here?"

"Tonight."

"Tonight? Ok cool. Same plan?

"Yup. You know what to do."

"Yes ma'am, no worries. I'll be seeing you tonight then."

"Yes you will boo," Avionne smiled, grateful for Payton's undying loyalty.

She hadn't seen or spoken to Payton in years. Payton was one of her adopted cousins and the two of them had naturally clicked when they were smaller. They lost contact after Payton graduated high school. She was a little older than Avionne and had left for nursing school, which is the one thing that came in handy when Avionne was in this latest crunch. She hadn't trusted Harris during her entire pregnancy. She knew that he would ultimately pull some ookie-doke move and bless the baby monkey if she hadn't been right. She'd had Payton on stand-by for that purpose. Payton had transferred into Anne Arundel once

18

Avionne had been put on bedrest and the rest is history. *I'm always thinking ahead boo.* She knew that Harris continually underestimated her, which is something that she couldn't understand. For him to have such an obsession with her mother, he sure couldn't tell that the apple didn't fall far from the tree. She was constantly able to pull the wool over his eyes at every turn.

"Now please, tell me more about my gorgeous baby! I cannot wait to see him tomorrow."

"Oh, I can go on and on," Payton began gushing.

***

Sitting in the nursery, rocking Jaxon back and forth, as he read him a Mother Goose tale, Harris looked up when he heard a noise down the stairs. Checking the time on his watch, he saw that it was 3:30 in the morning.

"Hey babe, is that you?" Payton had said that she would be back in the wee hours of the morning.

"Yes boo, I'm coming up now," the familiar voice called out to him and his baby relaxed. Even though he knew that Avionne was locked up, sometimes he was still on edge. It wasn't that he was afraid of her; he had been in the force for over ten years. She was more so just an unsettling spirit to be around.

"Did you miss me?"

The hairs on the back of Harris' neck prickled when he heard that voice. The voice he was dreading, Jaxon's mother, Avionne.

Squeezing his baby tightly to him, Harris glared at Avionne.

"What are you doing here? I know for a fact that they didn't just let you walk out of that jail down there." Harris was pissed off. Avionne was like a roach. No matter how much you stomped on her, she seemed to reappear everywhere.

Avionne shrugged, "I had other plans. They'll be looking for me soon, so I won't stay to bother you. I just came to get my son and we can all go our separate ways."

"You'll want to do what she says. It's two of us and one of you. We will win." Harris gaze switched to Payton.

"What does our situation have to do with you? And what do you mean it's "two of us?" You're working with Avionne?"

Payton smiled. "How else do you think she got here? We always put family first."

"Family?" Harris whispered. "Y'all are related?"

"Now for a man who prides himself on research," Avionne began as she started approaching him. "You

21

sure didn't do your homework." As much as she loved banter, she didn't have time today. She had to get her child and get as far away from this place as she possibly could.

Harris held Jaxon closer. "You won't get away with this."

"Fuck," Avian took out her gun with a silencer attached to it and shot Harris in the head. She grabbed her son before he fell to the floor. "Didn't I tell you I didn't have time? Now look what you made me do," she scolded Harris' dead body. "You done gone off, and got yourself shot." She shook her head. "Men." She looked over at Payton in exasperation. "What is it that they expect us to do with them? We give them chance after chance and they still act a fool."

"I know," Payton said, nodding in agreement. "Here, take this bag. It has everything you need to get away from here and everything your son needs as well."

"You're not coming?" Avionne asked, as she reached for the bag, no time to enjoy the feel of her baby boy in her arms.

"No," Payton shook her head. "You go ahead. I'm going to stay here and deal with this mess. Try to give you more time to get to where you're going."

"I love you so much, you know that? You are the best cousin that a girl could ask for. You may be the only person in the world that I've said that to and meant it. I haven't even said it to Lucas yet."

"I love you more. Go on now. Get outta here. The people from everywhere gonna be looking for you soon."

"I know. Ok big cuz, I'm out. Catch you later." Avionne gave her a tearful smile as she turned to walk out the door. "Actually I probably won't."

Holding her son close in her arms, she bounded down the stairs, looked around before exiting the backdoor and blended in with the night.

Remi's Open Letter

I finally realize that I have to grow up. I'm going to trust Nathan and see if he upholds his word. I'm going to raise Luna with as much Shia, Leigh and, I can get into her. I'm going to be more responsible and actually look like someone's mother. I'm saying goodbye to my colorful hair, my excessive piercings, and my tattoos. Ok the tattoos may be taking it too far, but I'll cover some of them up every now and then. I still have to be me you know.

The kids are great. Thanks for asking. ;) The twins are doing their thing. You know boys will be boys ... getting more into girls and being grown. Luna is resilient. She's bounced back the fastest and she will right the deaths in our family. I honestly think she's too young to really understand. She keeps the rest of us happy because she's happy and fearless. Truth be told, we could all learn a thing or two from her. She's the greatest kid on earth.

Vacation has been fun, but now it's time to return to the real world. I have to get them some stability. However, we are done with Greensboro. I do believe I am going to take them all back to Maryland where my siblings and I grew up. That place has always felt like home to me. I love everything about it. The sounds, the air, the way you can have city life in D.C. at night but be on your suburban tip by day.

I need to go back to where love was. My mom may have driven me crazy, but I loved her for what it's worth. It's ironic how my sister's and my parents were murdered by one of my mom's ex-lovers and Luna's parents were killed by her dad's ex-lovers daughter. History was repeating itself. I'm a do my best to break the cycle. These children and I will survive. We are survivors. Life has thrown us so many punches that it can't help but give us some sunshine. I know in my heart that there is a rainbow shining over a mountain somewhere with our names on it. And dog gon it I am going to find that mountain for us. I'm not saying I'm trying to be anyone's Mother Theresa, I don't plan on saving the world or anything, but please believe I'm going to save what's left of my family and that's just gonna be what it's gonna be.

Whether you like, love, hate me or have no opinion of me, know this ... it is finally Remi's turn to shine and I fully intend to do so. By any means necessary.

Remi

He Loves Me,
He Loves You Not 5

Remi's World

Finally it is my turn, my story. I've been waiting a long time for this moment, one that I will cherish. You thought you had an idea, but you really don't. No one knows what it has been like being me. The younger sister of twins. The forgotten one. Sure, they loved me as best they could, but never like they loved one another. There's was a secret world that only they could enter, a twin world. I tried tapping at the door a few times, but to no avail. They try to make me feel included, but they shared a bond that I could never penetrate. And here I am, left alone. Both sisters gone, they couldn't even live without one another. The cosmos took care of that. Even now, in death they are together. Now it is my time. The baby sister. The only one. Welcome to my world. A world of one. Shall we begin...

~Remi

CHAPTER | 1 the past

Drifting out of sleep as the smell of Chanel No 5 entered her room, Remi braced herself for the inevitable in her sleepy state.

"Remi darling, you must arise, it's time for school," Alicia joyfully announced as she entered Remi's black painted bedroom; crossing it to open the black cotton curtains that hung from heavy copper rods to let sunlight in and give the room a cheery pick me up.

Remi groaned at the ray of light shining brightly through her room. Pulling the white comforter over her head, she was on the verge of tears when the light continued to penetrate through the comforter and her sealed eyelids.

"Mother, please go away." Her sleep laced voice muffled by the comforter. She wasn't in the mood for Alicia's high strung, bipolar personality today. Her royal highness could be a lot to deal with.

"Come now little missy," Alicia droned on as she entered the room. "You know Mother isn't one for debates. Now get up."

Responding to the sternness in Alicia's voice, not wanting things to go from good to bad, Remi sighed loudly to make her irritation known as her eyes slowly opened and she kicked the comforter off her weary body. Rising as quickly as her body would allow, she gazed at her mother who was waiting expectedly at her bedroom door.

"Ma'am, I'm up."

Alicia's stern face broke into a smile. "Great!"She beamed at Remi. "I have your favorite blueberry waffles, bacon, and eggs ready for you on the table downstairs. So let's hop to it."

Remi gave her a semi-smile as she willed her eyes to focus solely on the pretty, petite woman in front of her. Her mother had an infectious smile that was radiant. Moments like this when she was acting like a normal mother and not a psycho person, she wasn't half-bad.

"Thanks Ma."

"Oh darling no fuss now." Alicia waved her hands as if brushing away the thank you. "I can't have you going to school malnourished now can I?" she asked as she walked out the room.

Remi sighed in relief and shook her head as the perfume drenched diva beauty queen exited her space.

Today wasn't bad at all. She thought, as she made her way downstairs in her pajamas.

"Have you packed?" Her mother asked as soon as she entered the kitchen and Chanel No. 5 hit her nostrils.

"Yes Ma'am," Remi replied, as she sat at the kitchen table and poured syrup over her blueberry waffles.

"I don't see why you feel as if you have to run up to New York every weekend to see your sisters. You could stick around here and keep me company sometimes you know. Maybe we could hang out or something."

Taking her time in responding, Remi returned the syrup to the table. Lifting her gaze to meet her mother's she wondered since when did this diva want to 'hang out'? This was a new development. Alicia normally enjoyed her alone time.

"I apologize mother. I was unaware that you were in the business of hanging out with your children."

"Well," she paused. "I know," Alicia replied as she walked over to Remi and placed her hands in her hair gently running her fingers through its long length. "I just like the company these days. Ever since your sisters moved up there, they rarely call or visit. And with you gone every weekend almost the house seems unusually large and much to empty."

Remi wasn't sure whether to barf now or later. *Ma has to be experiencing a midlife crisis.* Opting not to say anything in response, she resumed eating her breakfast as the diva continued to play with her hair.

***

"Remi, I'm sorry that I can't pick you up. You'll have to meet me at the hospital. Leigh's been in a fight." Shia spoke softly to Remi through her cell trying to be as quiet as possible since she wasn't supposed to have her phone in the area.

"Leigh stay in some mess. Now I have to fend for myself. Which hospital are y'all at?"

"I'll text you the address." Shia whispered. "I have to go. See you in a few."

"You know Ma is here right?" Remi mumbled to Shia as she entered the room. "I have no idea how

37

she managed to get her before me and she had no intention of coming to New York this weekend.

Shia stood up to give Remi a hug. "I'm so glad you made it. Where did you see Ma?"

"Out in the hall." Remi replied. "She is causing all types of havoc around here trying to locate Leigh."

Shia shook her head. "Seeing Ma when she wakes up is the last thing Leigh needs."

"Who you telling? I can go out there and try to deter her for a little while." Remi offered.

"That would be great." Shia gave Remi a grateful smile glad that her sister was here to help.

Sensing movement an hour later, Shia glanced up at the hospital bed from the chair she had been sleeping in for the last day. She saw Leigh fidgeting around and immediately jumped up to assist her.

"Lei Lei, be careful. You don't want to hurt yourself any more than you have too."

"What happened to me?" Leigh managed to creak out.

Gently brushing Leigh's wild hair off her face, Shia winced looking down at her. The left side of Leigh's face had been sliced up, bitten and bruised so badly that a bystander would never believe they were identical twins.

"You got your ass beat."Remi loved being a smart ass to Leigh. It was something that she just couldn't help not indulge in. Leigh was such an easy target.

Shia narrowed her eyes and shook her head at the comment their younger sister Remi had made. Leave it to her to "gently" break the news.

"Thanks Remi," Shia sarcastically began. "I'll take it from here."

"Suits me." Remi shrugged.

Staring into Leigh's swollen eyes, Shia attempted to smile.

"That bad huh?" Leigh's raspy voice asked.

"Well," Shia began slowly. "Not technically that bad, but you look beaten up a little. What happened? You want to talk about it?"

Remi wanted to say something, but opted to bite down on her tongue instead to keep quiet.

Leigh went to shake her head and then thought better of it when she felt the pain begin in her face.

"Umm, you gonna have to think of something because Ma is in the hall about to have a heart attack. Remi spotted her out there a few moments ago."

"Ma is here?" Leigh was shocked. It wasn't like their mother to drop everything and be by her bedside. She was selfish like that.

40

"Why?"

"What do you mean why? Because she's our mother."

"Shy; please don't take up for her. She gives selfish a whole other name."

"I'm not taking up for her. I'm stating the facts. She is "our" mother."

"Spare me this conversation please. I just want to rest." Leigh said, leaning into her pillows. She fell into her own thoughts, highly upset that Sherri had put her into the hospital. This war was far from over. Sherri was going to get hers.

The hospital door suddenly banged open and Leigh could smell her perfume before she fully entered the room and spoke.

"Oh My God! My baby! Are you ok? Can you breathe? You look so terrible!"

Leigh's eyes rolled beneath closed lids. She wasn't in the mood to stomach her mother's irritating antics today.

"What happened to my baby?" Shia moved to the side as their mom almost trampled over her to get to the side of Leigh's bed. Remi let out a disgusted sigh and left the room.

"Leigh, baby can you hear me?"

Shia almost laughed aloud as she observed Leigh pretending to be asleep. Leigh should pursue an acting career; she was definitely a comedic sight. Leigh displayed no signs of being sleepy only a few seconds before their mother burst through the door. Now she had her eyes shut, her mouth was slightly open, and she'd managed to be drooling. It was truly a pitiful sight to see.

"Ma, I think Leigh needs her rest right now. Why don't you come back later, once she's awake?"

Turning to gape at Shia as she spoke, their mother had a surprised look in her eyes.

"Shia, baby," her mother began, while kissing the air above her forehead. "I didn't see you standing there."

Considering that she had practically knocked her over to get to Leigh's bed, Shia found that hard to believe and chose not to respond. That was their mother, a dramatic ex-beauty queen diva. Like Remi and Leigh, Shia harbored very strong negative feelings toward their mother, but she tried to be the peacemaker between them all.

"Ok, baby," her mother said, pushing past her in a transparent cloud of perfume, "I must go now, people to see, things to do. Muah!" Blowing air kisses as she strolled out the hospital room.

"Thank the Lord that crazy woman has gone away."

Shia turned back towards the bed at the sound of Leigh's voice and smiled at her.

"You are such a trip. How could you possibly not want to let our mother coddle you? It was a once in a lifetime opportunity and you missed out." Shia's voice oozed with sarcasm.

"Shy; please don't make me throw up. I'm too old at this point. I no longer need a mother. I have you and Remi, so I'm good. Speaking of which, where is Remi?"

"She stepped out when Ma sashayed in."

"I'm right here," Remi announced from the door. "I can't stand that lady sometimes. I left to get a breather. Since you two have moved out she has been all up in my grill. I can't do anything anymore. Y'all need to come back and rescue me."

"When can I get out of here? I'm ready to go."

"We can check you out whenever you're ready."

"Good," Leigh said, shoving the covers off her. "Let's be out." She attempted to sit up and screamed in pain.

Shia and Remi both ran to her to help her sit up the best she could.

"What did that bitch do to me?"

"You have a few bruised ribs. You got beat up pretty badly. Your whole body will be sore for a while."

"Damn," Leigh mumbled.

Shia looked at her intensely. "You sure you don't want to talk about it?"

45

"No Shy, I do not want to talk about it."

"I don't blame you boo." Remi chimed in, "I wouldn't want to talk about getting my ass beat either. I mean how embarrassing."

"Remi," Shia began in a stern tone. "Cut it out. You see that she's been through a lot, give it a rest."

"Ok, I won't say anything after I just say this one last thing," she paused for dramatic effect. "Leigh you look like shit," she said, as she burst out laughing.

Shia closed her eyes and shook her head. Teenagers, what can you say they will be who they are.

"Remi, you only got so much to say because you see me in this bed. Don't make me get up and hurt you."

Remi began to laugh even harder. "The same way you hurt whoever did this to you. Girl stop."

"Ok, enough. Both of you stop it. Remi go out to the desk and check Leigh out. Leigh, let's get your clothes on so we can get out of here."

Whatever. Remi thought. Shia once again was taking on the role of mother, when they still had one alive and kicking in the very same hospital matter of fact.

As Remi exited the room with no further commentary, she just wanted to hurry and get Leigh checked out before their mother returned. Stopping at the nurse's station to get her sister's paperwork, they were ready to head back uptown.

"She's all checked out let's go before Ma returns." Remi announced as she bounded back into the   room.

CHAPTER | 2 the present

Nate has been a godsend. Because having never been a mother and being thrown into the role of caregiver; these kids can make one lose their mind fooling with them and become an alcoholic of sorts. How does anyone want to become a mother, especially a single one? It's not that they're bad; it's just that with four of them I'm ready to pull out my hair. The last four years have been very interesting. There's been no sign of Avionne's drama where she could be lurking in the shadows waiting to jump out at us or something to that effect; we are living ok. They still have us in the witness protection program. But that's okay because Nate continues to be like a guardian angel and my soul mate. I haven't trusted a guy since my whole fiasco with Shia's deceased husband Demitri. The inhuman torture that he put me through was enough to make no woman want to be with any many ever, but Nate was changing all of that. He is changing me.

Demitri made me hate men. It's been many years that he's been dead. I can't even remember how many and I still have a hard time letting go of what happened to me and what he forced me to do. That is until Nate came to show me the way. He's taught me how good it can be when a man loves you. Like really loves you. He helps me with the kids, he cooks for me, he massages my feet when I've had a long day and I'm tired, he helped me get my online company off the ground. Everything is great. But it scares me. We have no drama I always feel as if something is lurking in the background, trying to steal my joy, or that one day I'll wake up and he will be gone away from me like a mystical creature in a fairytale.

I completely went off on a tangent, back to the kids. They are all grown now. The twins moved out and were doing the grown up thing. Joelle was a teenager and doing the normal teenage thing, trying to outsmart the witness protection people. Just being crazy and insane. And then there was Luna, the apple of my eye, thus the whipped cream on my strawberry shortcake. She was everything to me. I tried not show favoritism toward her, but she's the one that didn't know what it was like to have a mother and father the most. She's so young that she doesn't even remember who they are anymore, which is a very bad thing; very bad. I show her as many photos as I can and tell her that her parents loved her beyond a shadow of a doubt, but she just glances at the photos as if to appease me only and moves on to the next thing uninterested.

Every day I think about my sisters and wish that they were still around. I miss Leigh even though we used to fight like cats and dogs, she always understood me the most. Shia was a little different. Always trying to be Leigh and I mother as if we didn't know any better. Even though she could irk my soul

51

sometimes trying to be another mother and though they both peeved me in their own ways, I miss my sisters. I would just like to know in what world is it okay to leave the baby of clan alive, take her sisters and make her a mother of four all in the same breath? This is just crazy man. I'm a totally different person now. Gone are my completely eccentric days. The days of wild colorful hair and potty mouth. These days I go to soccer games, PTA meetings, my hair has grown out, and it is now one solid color. Brown. I cover my tattoos and actually shop at New York & Company to try to look like a respectable woman. It's all so crazy how life has turned out. If you would have told me ten years ago that I would be parading around town as the mother of four kids, I would have laughed in your face. Look at me, that's my reality and I'm out here doing it and succeeding at it, and for this I am grateful.

"Hey beautiful," Nate placed soft kisses on the side of Remi's neck.

Jumping slightly from the unexpected kiss that interrupted her thoughts Remi turned and smiled at Nathan.

"Hey there mister. What are you doing here so early?"She asked.

"I got off work early and I was anxious to see you," he told her.

"Oh yeah, so what are you anxious to see me for?"

"So I can get some kisses," Nate told her as he looked down into her brown eyes.

He knew that after four years, being with Remi was definitely a conflict of interest for his job and for him to do his job effectively. But he also knew there was something magnetic about her. He always wanted to be close to her at any cost, even his job. Finally, his Chief had relented and told him that as long as it didn't interfere with his work then it shouldn't be too much of a problem. Nate made it a point to keep his professional life and his work life separate and he was still one of the head people in charge of the witness protection program for our children and me.

"Is that right?" Remi asked as she looked into his chocolate eyes.

"That is absolutely right," Nate smiled at her.

Remi knew that she had definitely won the lottery where Nate was concerned he was exactly what dreams are made of, exactly. She knows that this is God's way of repaying her for the time that she suffered at Demitri's hands.

Gently lifting her chin up so that he could lean down, he began to kiss her with all the love that he felt in his heart. He knew without a doubt that this was the woman he wanted to spend the rest of his life with. And he had a huge surprise coming her way in a few weeks. All he had to do was pick up the ring from the jeweler.

"Auntie RiRi! Auntie RiRi!" Breaking off the kiss from Nate after hearing her baby calling her from the hall, she patiently waited for and offered up an apology to Nate with her eyes. He was super patient. What other man would accept a woman with four children that she was raising that weren't hers?

"Auntie RiRi!"

"Yes, baby girl, what's going on?"Luna came running into the room.

"Guess what?" Remi automatically smiled from the excitement in her voice.

"What little lady?"

"Look what I found on the ground."

Remi braced herself. She never knew with this one. Luna was the non-typical outdoorsy wildlife one in the family.

"I'm almost scared to see."

"Oh come on Auntie, don't be a 'fraidy' cat."

Nate smirked as he watched their interaction in front of him. He loved the way she let him handle the children. She was a far cry from the woman he first met on the beach. That woman had piercings coming out of every part of her body, shaved hair that was colorful and went into a Mohawk, and tattoos galore. She always had a nice spirit, but her outward appearance was toned down now. And he knew that

that was all because of the children. She was attempting to be the best she could be for them and that's what he loved about her; her unselfish heart.

"I am NOT a 'fraidy cat girl. Let me see what's in your hands." Remi laughed.

Luna smiled as she came to stand right under her and pushed her hands in her face.

Remi almost threw up when she saw the worm wiggling around Luna's hands.

"Oh that is so gross." Remi frowned up her face not in the least excited about what Luna was holding in her hands.

"It's not gross. Here touch it." Luna demanded pushing her hands closer and closer to Remi's face.

Remi was horrified.

"Luna, let me see. I'll hold it." Nate told her letting Remi of the hook. She shot him a grateful smile. Thank you she mouthed.

Nate returned her smile, "Anytime beautiful."

Luna promptly walked over to him and Nate took the worm out of her tiny hands. Remi appreciated a man's man and Nate was definitely that.

CHAPTER 3 the past

It's time for them to say goodbye. They cannot exist in my world. I should never have left one alive and the kids too. None of them deserves to be here and I plan to have my way.

"Okay, I'm ready," she told the doctor. Glancing at her reflection one more time in the mirror for a few moments longer. Feeling her eyes begin to moisten, she quickly looked away from the mirror. I'm about to wipe all traces of Phylicia away. I can do this.

Avionne lay down on the table and closed her eyes as the doctor began to administer the medicine.

When Avionne woke a short time later her face felt as if someone had taken a shovel and beat her in the head with it.

The bandages were wrapped around her face tightly. And even though she was comfortable because of the medicine, she knew once the medicine wore off, her face would feel like it was killing her alive.

"There you are. You should be good to go in a few weeks." The doctor informed her.

"And will I look like the photo I showed you?" Avionne inquired.

"Yes ma'am you will," the doctor told her.

"Wonderful." Avionne was elated and she attempted a smile with her face bandaged.

Knowing that she would be looking strange for a few weeks, she wondered how her toddler would take it. She didn't want to scare him, but she didn't know what else to do.

Lucas was two years old now. And she was so thankful for him every day. When she knocked out this last job, she would dedicate the rest of her life to just being his mother. She had to change his name so that he would be Lucas, his father had originally named him Tim Jackson. Avionne had it changed back to Lucas and now he was a thriving little, chubby, black haired boy running around talking her head off. She loveed him more than life itself. After becoming a mother she had even less sympathy for

Phylicia because she couldn't understand how a mother could leave her baby behind, or give her away, or not check on her for years to chase another man. There wasn't a man alive that could make Avionne leave her son. Not one. She would go down in a blaze of fire first.

She was glad that the doctor had been able to come to her home and do this procedure. She was in her own bed resting nicely. Her cousin Payton had come to help her through the few weeks it would take her to recover. Payton had taken Lucas out for some ice cream and would be returning with him shortly. In the meantime, Avionne decided to take nap.

"Mommy," Are the words Avionne woke up to as her son came bouncing into the room. "Auntie Payton took me to get ice cream."

Lucas attempted to jump on the bed as Avionne leaned up, but once he caught a glimpse of her face, he immediately fell back in terror and began to cry.

Payton quickly ran to his side. "It's okay Lucas honey," she stated. She bent down and scooped them off the floor. "It's mommy."

Lucas kept shaking his head no, as the tears came down.

"It's okay honey, it's a mommy. My face is just wrapped up."

Once he heard her voice, Lucas stopped crying and just looked at her trying to find traces of the mommy that he knew.

"Mommy?" He whispered

"Yes honey it's me."Trying to reassure him as he squiggled out of Payton's arms and made his way to the bed looking up at her curiously.

63

"What happened?"

She didn't know what to say to him. *How do you explain to a child that you literally had your face taken off and a new one put on, well not actually, but you know what I mean.* I changed all my features to no longer look like myself so I will never look like the mommy he recognized. *He will only recognize my voice from now on.*

Picking Lucas up slowly trying not to hurt herself, she touched his hands to make sure they didn't touch her face. "Mommy is not feeling well," she explained to him as to the reason why my face is as it was.

Lucas sighed as he continued staring at her as if trying to make sure that she wasn't lying to him and really was his mother.

"See Lucas there's nothing to be afraid of," Payton interjected as she watch the two. "Do you think the doctor did a good job?"

"Only time will tell," she said as she continued to hold her baby boy who was still trying to figure out if he could trust her.

If the doctor did his job correctly then I should look exactly like the picture I've given him. About to set the world on fire and they don't even know yet.

Payton smiled as she watched her, "I'm so glad I'm your cousin. Cuz I would not want to be on your bad side."

"Please remember that for future reference," Avionne said. As they continued to watch Lucas, who had finally decided that Avionne was who she said she was, and he laid his head on her chest, and relaxed his body.

"I love this little crumb snatcher so much."

"I know you do." Payton told her. "So are you ready to set everything in motion?" Payton asked.

"Not exactly." Avionne told her. "I want to make sure that my face is okay and then we'll go from there."

"Okay you're the boss," Payton told her as she left the room.

Avionne would have smiled if her face weren't in bondage like a mummy. *What did I ever do to deserve her*, she thought.

CHAPTER | 4 the present

Looking down at her four-year-old son Lucas, she couldn't believe how fast the years were passing by. It seemed like only yesterday she was pregnant with him and then had his father Harris attempt to take him from her and go to jail and breaking out. All of that within a period of two months she just couldn't understand how now she actually had a four year old running around, talking her head off, leaving his toys all over the living room, and doing everything but what he was supposed to be doing. He began talking back but Avionne allowed it. This was the first time in her life that she had allowed anyone to run their mouths back to her. But Lucas was just so cute you just couldn't resist the urge of pinching his little cheeks. What with his milk chocolate skin color, his curly hair, and his brown eyes; he was the apple of her eye and she loved apples.

"Girl what are you in here doing?"Payton asked her.

Avionne glanced up at her, "Nothing much, just thinking about Lucas, and how big he had gotten. I miss my little baby."

Payton laughed, "Well you know what they say, that means it's time to have another one."

"Another what girl? You tried it." Avionne told her. "I am NOT having any more babies. If I did that would mean I would have to get a husband or boyfriend or let some man into my life and I don't have time for that right now."

"Girl please with all this new technology, you don't need a man for anything. You can take yourself right onto that sperm bank, get you some A one prime delicious sperm, and have anybody's kids that you want."

"As exciting as that sounds P, I can't. With the life that I live, I really don't want to bring a baby into that situation. Lucas was a blessing and I love him but we don't need any more little people anytime soon.

Especially now that the plan is in motion and about to take off. I just can't have it any other way."

"This is true. But I just wanted to let you know that you do have options and you're not stuck if you want to have more kids have them."

"I hear what you're saying, but like I said previously, it is easier said than done. My life is too crazy and it is not conducive for any children. Lucas is the love of my little life, the light at the dark tunnel that I have, he's my reason for being alive. I think that's why I was so angry with my own mother. I have to find my own reason like I was searching for something I was dealing with her because it gave me a purpose in the world, but now that I have Lucas, he is my purpose, he is my reason, and I don't need anything but him."

"This is true. I was just making some suggestions. You can do whatever you want."

"I know this." Avionne said to her, "but I do appreciate your input, in case I don't tell you enough. You're definitely appreciated and I love you."

And what amazed Avionne is that she really did love Payton. Payton has stuck in her corner and she rode all these years with her as if everything was cool. She hadn't been judgmental, she always did what she was told, she never asked many questions, and Avionne respected her for that. Anybody that can handle business, keep their mouth closed, and do what they're told and leave you alone and not cause problems was the best person to have in your corner. Plus Payton also made a lot of money being a nurse and money is something Avionne definitely needed. Being on the run for four years was a lot to handle and she didn't have many resources when it came to money because everything involved with her name, her mother's name, her family have been flagged in the off chance that she would come out of hiding. She also couldn't put Lucas in any pre-K or kindergarten because the feds were looking for him as well. You have no idea how hard it is to keep a child cooped up for four years. It's as if he doesn't know what the world is like. He doesn't get to go outside and play like normal kids, he has to be in the house, and Payton is his best friend in the world. Sometimes Avionne would feel bad because she felt as if she couldn't give him the life he deserved to have and that was her fault. He also was growing up without a father, which was also her fault. She had single handedly taken everything that would be important to him away except for her and she didn't know if that was a good or bad thing.

"Well I'm definitely feeling this new look you got going on." Payton told Avionne.

Laughing at her cousin, Avionne responded, "Payton it's been two years since I've looked like this. What are you talking about?"

"I know but you look good. I think you should finally test it out in the world, like I think it's time for you just to see what you can do."

"It is time, and I'm trying to really figure out what it is that I want to do. It has taken me two years to adjust to looking like this."

Payton grunted "I am surprised that you did something so drastic. I thought you were just going to change your cheek bones or your mouth something

73

small, but you change your entire face to look like someone else."

"I know and that's what got me so crazy. I've had to look at myself in the mirror every day and get used to this face like some days I scare myself because I don't know, I think I'm looking at her, and I'm like what is going on this is craziness."

"Well yeah kinda is," Payton agreed. "But you did what you felt like you needed to do so I say let's just roll with it you know."

"That's easier said than done. And it is easy for you to say something like that since it was not your face that had to be changed, it was mine."

"I know. I'm just trying to sympathize with you I know I don't really understand what it is like to go through what you going through but I'm just trying to understand Avi. I'm just trying to understand."

"Well thank you so much for being so understanding I really do appreciate it. And I really do appreciate all you've done. Also you gave your life for me and Lucas, and that in itself is amazing and I'm so thankful that you're my cousin."

"You never have to thank me for that."

"I know but I just want to."

"Okay that's fine." Payton smiled at her. "Are you ready to talk about what we're going to do now?"

"Absolutely. You're right. It is time for me to go out into the world I do know that the family has moved back to their hometown in Maryland so it may just be time to pay them a visit. Lucas is looking forward to finally being able to have a road trip, so I know he'll be pretty excited. We just have to be extra careful," Avionne said as she gazed into Payton's eyes. "That means we cannot travel together we can't be seen together we have to act like the other doesn't exist."

"I know." Payton told her I've already scouted out a place for us to stay so that once you come; we'll be good to go. I'm transferring back to Anne Arundel and we'll go from there."

"I really don't think you should go back to Anne Arundel. I really want go to Baltimore and you can go to John Hopkins. It's a great hospital great experience and just a different atmosphere."

"I don't know anything about Baltimore."

"You'll learn." Avionne told her. "So we will be going to Baltimore instead and then you will commute to the city. It is not that far, like 45 minutes down to 95 on a good day highway 97 takes about 15 minutes on even better day."

Payton just shook her head, "How do you know all this stuff?"

"I make it my business to know everything there is to know about everything. It could be a matter of life and death, and that is something I can't afford. I am a research goddess. If I can read it, Google it, whatever I make it a point to do so. And if you're going to live this life with me you should really start to do the same."

"Okay. I will make it my business to do that from now on."

"Good. That's all I needed to know. I will begin a new life this week. You start trying to get transfered and I will begin looking for housing in Baltimore and Lucas and I will move down in about two weeks."

"Okay sounds like a plan. I will definitely get on that sooner than later."

"Perfect. That's exactly what I needed to hear."

There will be no survivors. Let the games begin.

CHAPTER | 5 the past

Waking from a cold sweat, she sat up abruptly in the dark room knowing that something wasn't right. She stretched out her arm to reach for the light on her nightstand.

"You don't need to bother with the light," a deep male voice informed her.

Remi felt the tears begin in the back of her eyes. Demitri had returned.

She watched the shadowy object come closer.

"Move over and don't say a word."

Remi wanted to scream out so bad, but her pride wouldn't allow it. She refused to ever let this man see her beg or see her screaming for help or in pain.

"What do you want?" she said defiantly.

Demitri's deep voice laughed. "You know what I want and I mean to have it."

"You have a wife. Why don't you go to her? I don't want you. Why would you continuously take someone when you have a wife willing to sleep with you every night?"

"Because I want you. You're young, fresh, sweet, and anytime I can have you, I'm going to take it."

"I want you to leave me alone. I don't want anything to do with you."

"Too bad. What you want isn't up for discussion."

"I will tell Shia."

"No you won't. Who do you think Shia is going to believe you or her husband?"

"My sister would believe me. She's that type of woman.

"Not if I tell her that you've been coming on to me, and messing with me, and walking around in those tiny little outfits that you do every day.

"What are you talking about? This is my everyday style."

"I know and I love it. You're so bold and beautiful."

"I'll become ugly then."

"I've already tasted the nectar. Nothing you do will ever turn me away." Demetri told her.

Remi hated her life. Why did sister marry this loser? With all the crap their family had been through, she knew news about her husband would break Shia, and she didn't have the heart to hurt her sister, no matter how much of a monster her brother-in-law was. Shia deserved to be happy. Remi and Leigh owed so much to her. She was like a mother to them.

"I hate you so much. One day you're going to get yours."

Demitri laughed in her face. "And who's going to give it to me you? Right now?"

Remi closed her mouth upset that he could turn anything sexual and she hated him with every cell in her body.

"I love you. Don't you see that?"

Remi laughed aloud. "You're comical. You have no idea what love is. You wouldn't know love if they hit you in the head with a bat. I don't know why you married Shia because you don't love her. I feel like this is a nightmare and I want to get out of it."

"There is no getting out of it. I'm here to stay and you will do what I tell you to do." Remi shook her head as the tears rolled down her face.

She wanted out so bad, but once again, she refused to scream so this was just another long night. She knew he liked the scratches that she would angrily leave on his back, but it was her only way of inflicting pain on somebody who had broken her down, killed her spirit, hurt her soul, and forced a wedge in between the person she loved the most in the world. There was no turning back now. She knew she would be Demitri's slave forever unless she could figure out a way to get out of this house.

The next day

"Hey Remi, you ok? You seem so distant lately. Is everything okay?" Leigh asked her.

"No everything is not okay I hate living here."

"Oh is that all? I guess you gotta find somewhere else to live then."

"Oh Leigh, it's so bad. I hate Demitri."

"Girl join the club. I don't know what Shia sees in him. I think that whole Trent thing messed her up and she just went right along with the next guy who was really interested in her. Because I can't stand Demitri's ass either. He's a loser. There is something I don't like about him."

"I know. He's such a creep." Remi opened her mouth to tell Leigh about Demitri's nightly rape sessions when he walked into the kitchen."

"Hey ladies, what's going on?"

Leigh refused to answer as she turned and left the kitchen.

That was typically the gist of those two's relationship. Demitri spoke to her and she walked away.

"I didn't walk in on you about to tell your sister something she doesn't need to know that I?" Demitri asked.

"Not at all. You walked in on me leaving."

"Oh you're not going anywhere."

"Excuse me. Who are you to tell me where I can and can't go?"

"Your lover."

"Lover? Hardly. You are delusional is what you are."

"You are coming with me. I need to go somewhere."

"I really could care less where you need to go. I just know that I'm not going."

Demitri strolled over to Remi, placed his hands around her throat, and applied pressure.

Remi's eyes grew wide as she frantically swatted at his hands to try to loosen their hold on her.

"There, I finally have your attention. You are coming, you don't have a choice, and I don't want to hear anything else about it." He leaned his head in close so that he could whisper in her ear. "I will kill you. It would do you well to remember that at all times."

Remi closed her eyes as she tuned him out and turned her focus to breathing. He was applying so much pressure she felt as if her body was about to go limp.

He abruptly let go so that she could breathe. "Don't forget what we spoke about."

"Meet me at the car in five," Demetri said as he left the kitchen.

"I should kill him in his sleep," Remi thought, but immediately dismissed the thought. She would never be able to do something like that too Shia, not in a million years.

CHAPTER | 6 the present

"I mean how many soccer games do we have to go to?" Joelle asked with an attitude. "When will this be over? I have other things that I can be doing."

"Oh yeah, like what? Going to the mall?" Remi sighed. "We will go to as many games as Luna has.

Why do we go through this every Saturday morning? I don't understand. You know we're going to go to a soccer game you know that's what it is. I don't understand why we have to talk about this and you have to give attitude every single Saturday morning you need to get over it." Remi was tied. She gave Joelle the same speech every Saturday morning.

"Whatever." Joelle put her headphones on and began bopping to her music.

It was days like today that Remi wished she had been a better teenager to her mother. She knew this was nothing but karma coming back to bite her in the ass. Because it was taking everything in her not to smack the headphones off Joelle's head.

"Auntie RiRi, can I have some tacos for dinner?"

Remi was grateful to Luna. She was oblivious to everything, just living a kid's life.

"Sure pumpkin." Remi responded turning her attention to Luna. "We can stop by a restaurant to get some tacos."

"No. I like when you make them. Can we go to the store?"

"You just want to go to the store to try to talk me into buying you some candy. The answer is No. Before we even get there do you understand?"

"Yes auntie I understand. I'm not going to ask for candy."

"Ok. Then we'll stop by the store and get you some tacos since you played such a great game today. Three goals –that's everything."

Remi looked through the rearview mirror to see Luna smiling at her. God I adore this kid.

As the trio were leaving the grocery store, Remi did a double take. She didn't know if her eyes were playing tricks on her, or what was going on, but with everything in her being she could swear that her sister Shia was walking towards her.

"Shia?" She said to the woman as she was walking past her in the parking lot.

The woman smiled softly at Remi as she stopped.

"Hi, I'm sorry do I know you?"

Remi closed her eyes for a moment, the voice was different, but the face was the same. Even the birthmark Shia had on her face.

"Ma'am are you okay?" The woman asked concerned.

"I'm so sorry." Remi told the lady as she tried not to have a mini heart attack on the parking lot. "You look exactly like my older sister Shia that passed away four years ago."

"That is so weird." The lady informed her. "My name is Shia as well."

Remi had no idea if she has stepped into the twilight zone or what. Someone definitely had to be playing a trick on her.

"This is impossible," she told the lady. "We buried my sister with her husband."

"I'm so sorry to upset you, miss. But I don't have any sisters. It's just me. Well it's not true I did used to have one a long time ago but she died when she was five and it's been me by myself ever since."

"I'm so sorry to hear that," Remi told her. "You look so much like my sister if it's as if you are Shia, this is so strange. Like I don't know what to do part of me wants to pull you into a hug and embrace you and the other part is like what the hell is going on."

"I'm so sorry to upset you like this. But I'll be more than happy to give you a hug if that's what you need."

"No, that won't be necessary I just, I guess I'm just having a moment. I really miss her and it seems so out of place. Of all the grocery stores in the state I run into someone who looks exactly like my oldest sister Shia and your name is Shia as well. It's just weird."

Remi wondered if she was hallucinating. There was no way on God's green earth that the universe would be so cruel to bring this woman into her path.

"I'm sorry to do this to you. I hope you have a good day."

"I hope that you do the same as well," Remi told her.

As soon as they got home Joelle all but disappeared into the house and Nate came out to carry the groceries.

"You will never guess what happened to me today," she told him as soon as he was to the car, not even allowing Luna to get out yet.

"You're right I probably won't guess, so why don't you tell me," Nate said to her.

"I saw Shia."

"Shia? As in your deceased sister, Shia. That girl?"

"Well, not my sister Shia, but she looked like her I mean just like her. And get this her name is Shia. Like what are the odds of that happening? That I would be minding my business and run right into a Shia right there in the parking lot.

"That is a little suspicious," Nate said. "Things like that doesn't usually happen. And if they do happen, it makes me think that it is some sort of set up. I'm going to let my superiors know. But I think it's time that we put the rules back in place you're going to have to go back on very strict witness protection. I know we've relaxed the rules for you over the last couple of years because the threat didn't seem imminent, but now I'm not so sure. I'm going to investigate a little further. I don't want you to freak out and panic or anything. I just want you to be aware that danger does still exist for you and your family and is my job to stay on top of it and guarantee that you will be okay."

"I know honey and that's why I appreciate and love you so much. You are everything to me."

Nate's face broke into a grin. "I better be sexy. Now get in the house and take your clothes off."

Remi began laughing. "I cannot take my clothes off. I have got to fix dinner for those little crumbsnatchers in there."

"Fine, cook dinner then be in the bedroom in the nude right after."

"Oh, please believe me. You only have to tell me once." Remi laughed as she skipped into the house.

CHAPTER | 7 the past

"So why are you here?" a girl holding a brown stuffed teddy bear asked her.

"I live here now," Avionne told the girl.

"Really? What happened to your mommy and daddy?"

"My daddy died and my mommy is in jail. Well actually, in a hospital for the mentally and criminally insane."

"Wow. What kind of place is that?"

"I'm not entirely sure but I know she can't leave so it is like jail."

"She must of did something really bad to go to jail."

"She's a bad person, not very nice. I don't need her."

"Everyone needs a mommy." The girl said with sad eyes.

"I know. I guess that's why I'm here with you and your mommy."

"Yes, she is nice. She will take care of you."

"Well it may be nice to have someone care. "Avionne told her, "but it's not necessary. I've been learning to take care of myself."

"How can you possibly take care of yourself you're only eight?" The girl asked.

"I know a lot to be only eight years old. Age isn't anything but a number anyway. I'm way beyond my years trust me." Avionne informed the inquisitive girl.

"Oh, will you teach me some stuff?"

"Sure. First, you don't need to carry around a stuffed teddy bear it won't protect you. You have to learn how to protect yourself that's the way the world works. Even at eight I do know that much, toys are for kids."

The girl's eyes welled up in tears. "I have to give away my teddy bear?" she asked as her bottom lip begin to waiver. "I need my teddy."

"No you don't and you can't hang with me if you want to hang with the teddy," Avionne told the girl and then walked away from her.

A few moments later, she heard footsteps behind her and turned to see a young girl who was without a teddy bear.

"Where's your teddy?"

"I threw him away, so I can hang out with you. You're, right I don't need him anyway."

"Good. Now we can be friends. My name is Avionne."

"I'm Kamilah."

"Nice to meet you Kamilah. I've never had a friend before."

"Me either. We'll be like sisters."

"Sisters are cool I used to have one of those. She's dead now." Avionne told her.

"Your sister died? That's so sad. Well now we have each other."

"Yeah we do have each other and that's a great thing. Do you believe that bad people need to die?" Avionne asked her.

"Not really. I'm just a kid I don't think about dying I know it's a sad thing."

"Well, if you're going to hang with me you need to believe in dying. Sometimes you just have to let people go you know?"

"You can tell me more about it."

"Okay, I will."

CHAPTER | 8 the present

"**I** did it!" Avionne exclaimed as soon as she walked through the door of their new townhome in Baltimore.

"Oh yeah? So how did it go?" Payton asked her.

"It was like this crazy rush. I can't even put it into words. This is the best thing that ever happened. I ran into Remi and she didn't even recognize me. She mistook me for her sister Shia, which is exactly what I was going for." Avionne exclaimed.

"You are one sick cookie," Payton told her. "She really didn't recognize you?"

"No. She really thought I was her sister Shia. I'm going to have to go back and give that doctor a tip. He rocked my face out. I followed her to the grocery store, and when she got to the parking lot, I made it a point to walk past her at that very moment. When she saw me, she looked like she had seen a ghost. Like she almost lost her shit right there on the street. It was crazy."

"You seem to be enjoying this a little bit too much you really getting a rush out of this whole thing." Payton told her.

"I am." Avionne exclaimed, this is the first time she was able to see with this face can do. "I'm so excited."

"So you don't think it will seem weird or strange to people that grew up around here to see you walking around?"

"Well they always say that everyone has a look alike so who are we to judge. I'm just happy, but the plan is in motion, and we're about to begin new things. This is so exciting."

Payton stared at the excitement. In Avionne's face, she knew that she was dealing with a true sociopath or psychopath however this crazy chick could be classified. It didn't matter that she believed the Avionne just might fall into both categories. And that worried her. She wondered how safe she would be and how long she could keep this secret. It's not that she didn't love her cousin, she just didn't want anything bad to happen to Lucas, and Avionne who seemed to love the thrill of frightening and killing people and Payton wasn't really sure she was down for that anymore.

She really did want her to get it together and just be a mother. Now that she had this new face, she could do anything she wanted to do, be anyone she wanted to be. She didn't have to go back into a life of killing.

"Are you sure this is the route you want to take?"

"Payton you really crushing my high. What is the problem? Are you beginning to have doubts about what's going on here? You knew this was always the plan."

"No, I knew later on that this was the plan but in the beginning once you had the baby the initial plan was to go off and be happy being a mother I understand that two years later that changed, but I thought initially that Lucas would be enough to sustain your other urges.

Avionne shrugged, "Well you thought wrong. This is just something that I have to do."

"You know you seem to be more and more like your mother every day. The only difference is you are willing to kill the man that became a part of your life. Where that is something that your mother would have never done."

"Don't you dare compare me to my mother. If you're looking to get on my bad side that's the quickest way to do it." she narrowed her eyes beginning to see Payton in a brand new light.

"You have me second-guessing you now. And that's a very bad thing for you. I need to know that I can trust you, and if I feel for one moment that you can't be trusted, then I have to move on without you, and you have to be buried six feet under. Do you understand? Lucas loves you so much, I really would hate for some unfortunate accident to befall you. Think about it and let me know what it is you want to do."

"What exactly is that supposed to mean?"

"It means whatever you want it to mean but I'm being very serious with you Payton. You let me know what it is you want to do. You figure it out and let me know tonight."

With that, Avionne exited the room. Payton had effectively ruined her moment. Avionne had been on a high when she entered the house. Now she was going to have to figure out what to do about her. And she never worked well under pressure. She was beginning to understand her mother more and more. She could see why Phylicia rolled in a sole group of one. It was much easier to control what was and what would be that way.

She began whistling to herself as the wheels in her brain began spinning. *Seems as if my plan is going to need to be revised.* Family was risky and could be the worst sometimes.

CHAPTER | 9 the past

*D*emitri set me up. He did that to me on purpose so that I would have to be his puppet. How could I have a hand in kidnapping my sister? What am I supposed to say to Shia when she finds out and she will find out?

He had to find a way to blackmail me. That asshole made me ride with him to the airport. I had no idea what was goodnight, he just told me to stand there.

"Hey kiddo, where you been?"

Remi nearly jumped out of her skin at the sound of Shia's voice.

"Huh? What you mean? I've been here." She responded nervously.

"Here where? Why are you being weird?" Shia looked at Remi as if she were crazy, wondering what had her on edge. "Have you seen Leigh? She and I were supposed to go out this evening."

"Nope, haven't seen her have no idea where she is?"

Shia gave Remi a concerned look. "Rem you okay? Are you getting enough rest?"

"You know, I am a little tired. I think I will go lie down." Remi lied.

Shia gave Remi a sympathetic look. "You do that punkin. Love you."

"I love you too Shy."

"I know you do honey. Go get some rest. I'll talk to you later."

"Okay."

Remi retreated to her room to be alone with her thoughts.

Upon entering her room, she sensed that something was out of place. Cutting on the lights, she's saw Demitri sitting on her bed. "What are you doing in here?"

"I'm checking to make sure you didn't say anything to Shia about today."

"What exactly do you think I would say to her? Like how would I explain being there in the first place? There's no way to tell on you without telling on myself. I shouldn't have been there. You did this to me on purpose so you can blackmail me." She accused him.

"Turns out you are smarter than you look," Demitri told her with a smirk on his face. "I guess we have an understanding. Have a good night."

"I hate you."

"I love you too. You're the one sister that I love doing every night."

"You disgust me you nasty son of a bitch. Get out of my room right now." As soon as he walked out, Remi locked the door behind him, and shoved her bed in front of it. Tonight she will make sure that if anyone tries to get her room it would cause a commotion. There would be no shenanigans tonight. She was going to make sure of it.

Where is my sister? She began to worry again now that she was left to her own thoughts. She was concerned about Leigh's wellbeing. The whole thing had been staged. There were just too many people around and doing who knows what. Even Kodi and Trent had been there. For the life of her, she could not understand why all of them needed to be there when Leigh was kidnapped and she didn't understand why Leigh was kidnapped in the first place. Everything was just out of whack lately and Demitri was the cause of it. She had a feeling that Leigh must have been on to something. Because she was always suspicious of him, she wondered if that was what played into her being kidnapped today.

I just don't know what to do with everything. This is just too much information for one body to take in and I'm over all of it.

CHAPTER | 10 the present

"Will you marry me?"

Remi stood there in shock. She couldn't understand what was going on. One moment, she was standing there at the stove fixing spaghetti, the next moment Nate had walked in and was down on one knee proposing to her in the kitchen.

"Are you serious right now?" Remi asked him.

"I'm very serious. I want to spend the rest of my life with you. No one else just you."

Remi instantly felt the tears crashing down her cheeks. "The answer is yes. I need you with me at all times. I need to be with you. I love you. You're everything to me my savior. I've never met anyone like you and you saved me from hating men and from becoming a bitter old lady . You changed my cynical ways. You're so what I've been hoping for. You've taught me what love is, what truth is, for that, I'm grateful, and I love you."

Nate stood up in front of Remi and pulled her into his arms."Thank you. Thank you. I will spend the rest of my life making you the happiest woman on earth. Thank you for giving me the opportunity."

"I know. I trust you with my life, with my kids life just everything. I trust you to always be around; looking out for our family and that we're safe."

"You're my everything and I love you forever until the day I die." Nate told her.

"Thank you," Remi told him, as she watched him take out of the box a yellow canary ring and place it on her finger. Not sure what to say, she just leaned up and kissed every part of his face that she could reach.

"You make me very happy," he told her. "My life has been amazing since meeting you and you're amazing with the children. I've watched you grow into an amazing woman."

Remi blinked back tears. If only her sisters were here to see her now.

"Thank you for loving me and dedicating your life to making sure that my children and I are okay." She told him.

"You never have to thank me for that. I do what I need to do for the people I love."

"I know you do, which is why I'd be crazy to let you leave my life," Remi told him.

Nate smiled at her. "How about you retire with me for the evening?"

Remi smiled back up at him, "I thought that you would never ask." With Joelle and Luna in bed, they had nothing but space and opportunity.

Reaching up to pull his face down to meet hers, she took his mouth into hers and kissed him with all the love that she could muster up in her soul. This man was intoxicating and she wanted every inch of him.

Nate smiled into her kiss and swung her off her feet and into his arms. Taking the stairs two at a time, he made short work of getting them to the bedroom.

Lying her down, he gazed into his future wife's eyes as the moonlight shined across her face illuminating her body.

"I love you," he whispered into the night as he dipped his head and began kissing her neck.

Remi moaned softly. She loved anytime that Nate placed his hands on her. She was immediately turned on.

Hearing her moan was almost Nate's undoing. He found it amazing that he had been able to hang up his single card so readily upon meeting Remi.

She'd made him want to protect her and that included her heart. He'd never do anything to hurt the woman that he cherished more than his next breath.

CHAPTER | 11 the past

Avionne hated to say it but she loved her adopted mother Krista. Krista did everything she could to make Avionne one of the family.

Avionne appreciated that about her. Her own mother had never care one way or the other about her wellbeing and this was her first shot at a real family.

A true family. She loved Kamilah too. She wondered if she had let Khloe live, if the two of them would have been as close as she and Kamilah were now.

"What are you doing in here?"

Avionne looked up from the diary that she was writing in. "Scripting my thoughts. Sometimes it helps to see things on paper and to go from there."

"Oh ok." Kamilah smiled at Avionne. Over the years, the two of them had grown very close to one another. Meeting as children all those years ago, she was grateful that Avionne had entered her life. Avionne had taught her how to stick up for herself and not to believe in fairy tales ever because they never came true. She respected her for that.

"Do you want to come hang out with me? A few of us are going to the movies and then out to eat."

"No," Avionne told her. "I'd rather not. I have to begin planning out my future and what I'm going to do."

"Come on Avi, lighten up a little." Kamilah smiled at her. "You take life way too seriously sometimes. I wish that you would stop acting so grown up for once and have some fun."

Avionne stared at naive Kamilah as if she had two heads. Lighten up? She knew firsthand how lightless life could be. And she commended the way Kamilah tried to make the best of every situation, but she knew better.

"Life isn't as simple as all that Kamilah. I'd rather stay home, but you go and have a ball. I'd love to hear all about it when you return."

Kamilah sighed, "Okay. Love you Avi."

Avionne smiled at her. "I know, now get outta here."

"Okay. Later." Kamilah replied as she retreated from the doorway.

Returning her attention to her diary, Avionne realized that she was no longer in the mood to write anything.

Turning on her computer, she Googled her mother's name. She wanted to know where she was, how she was doing, and if she was still locked up. It was time to begin figuring out if she was going to seek her out. Even though she knew her mother didn't deserve it. Not like her mother had ever looked for her or anything.

Avionne read the screen, shocked to discover that her mother had broken out of the asylum years before and was somewhere on the loose.

The crazy woman has never even come to check

on me. She doesn't know if I'm alive or if I'm dead,

and what's even more, she doesn't care. All she ever

cared about was Khloe and Trent. That's why I had to

kill my little sister. Don't you see? I had to cancel out

the competition. Avionne thought about how peaceful

Khloe had looked at her funeral. I helped return her

to where she belonged. No one can understand that

but me. But she's exactly where she needs to be. Now

I have my own guardian angel. One that I have

picked myself, and one that I love. Despite what

people think even at such a young age, I did love

Khloe, but there was no way that the two of us to

coexist in the same world. Not when we were both

vying for Phylicia's attention and Khloe was the only

one receiving it.

Life just wasn't fair sometimes and Avionne was sorry that Khloe had to take it out for it. She shrugged, oh well, sometimes that's the way the cookie crumbles.

I'm not heartless, she opened her diary back up to pin her thoughts. She loved just like the next person. The only difference is she had been dealt a shitty hand and had no intention of living that way. She was going to create her own hand to live by.

"Avionne are you up here?"

"Yes I'm in here Krista." She yelled out.

"Oh there you are. You didn't want to go out with Kamilah and have some fun for once?"

"No I am ok in the room."

"You really have to get out more Avionne. I mean you're a teenager and you should be having fun not cooped up in the house all the time. You only get to be young once enjoy it."

"I do enjoy my life Krista. I just don't feel like I have anything in common with kids my age."

"That because you never go out to hang with them. You stay in the house all the time you don't even make an attempt to just hang out and have fun."

"They don't have the type of fun that I'm interested in."

"What kind of fun is it that you would like to have honey?" Krista asked her as she sat on the bed.

"Not their kind of fun," Avionne informed her. "I don't want to go to the movies and out to eat. There are more beneficial things that I can be doing with my time."

"You're seventeen. What else is there that you want to do? What do you think normal seventeen year olds are doing?"

"Well if I were normal, I do believe that I would be hanging out with Kamilah and her friends at the movies and going to dinner. But I'm anything but normal. I don't even know what normal is. I never have. My mother didn't raise me to be normal." As soon as the words left her mouth Avionne instantly regretted it once she saw Krista's wounded look.

"I thought I was doing a pretty good job of being your mom."

"I apologize Krista that's not what I meant. You're done a great job being my mom. But unfortunately my biological mother did such a bad job that I don't think I can ever get over something like that. Even though I do appreciate everything that you've done for me."

"I understand sweetie." Krista stood. "I do the best I can. I'll leave you be now."

"Thank you." Avionne watched a she exited her room. She knew that she had hurt Krista's feelings. She didn't mean to, but everyone in this house needed to come to grips with reality.

Avionne didn't intend to be the fun snatcher, but they all acted oblivious to what she was. And she was all about reality. She never stopped thinking about her previous life for one moment. Every day was count down to the day that she was to see her mother again face-to-face and nothing would deter her from her course of action.

CHAPTER | 12 the present

K nocking on the door, Avionne stood in front of the duplex that she had been watching for the past two years. Waiting patiently for the occupants to open the door, she ran her hands along her hair to make sure that it was hanging down flat and not a single hair was out of place.

A young male opened the door after a few moments. His face went as white as a sheet when he saw her face.

"Mom?" he whispered in shock.

Avionne smiled and nodded her head.

"What are you talking about?" Another male voice asked from behind. "Mom is dead. Who are you speaking to?"

The young man's twin came to the door and he too went white. "What the hell? Is this some kind of gross joke? Who are you?" He asked in disgust.

Avionne smiled, "Why your mother of course."

"Listen lady, I don't know what kind of game you're playing, but you are not our mother. You need to get out of here."

He attempted to slam the door in her face, but Avionne wedged her foot there to prevent it.

"My name is Shia."

The men both narrowed their eyes at her in unison then looked at each other then back to her.

"Please let me come in and explain."

Against their better judgment they stepped back skeptically and allowed her to enter. Once in the house with the door closed, Avionne pulled a gun out.

"What is wrong with you young people today? Don't you ask for identification or anything? You don't just let people in your house. I don't care how much they resemble someone that you know." she shook her head. "No child of mine would be this dumb."

"Who are you?"

"Oh no darling, question and answer time is over. You and your brother come sit over here nicely for mama." She smiled sweetly at them.

They really were handsome boys. A perfect mix of Shia and Demetri. They were her brothers. They had no idea who she was and she preferred it that way.

"I'm really sorry to involve you two in this mess, but your family is cursed and everyone must die." She shrugged as their eyes enlarged at her statement."It is just the ways of the world."

"You're going to kill us?"

"Absolutely," Avionne responded with no hesitation. "Now you two come sit on the sofa over here."

The two men obliged her.

"I apologize for this. It has nothing to do with you and everything to do with our parents. But when you get to heaven, please tell Khloe hi for me. I miss her." Avionne held back tears as she pulled the trigger on both the men, two quick shots to the head. One for each. Unscrewing the silencer, she left out the house the same way that she had entered. Returning home just in time to have dinner with her son.

What a great day, she thought.

CHAPTER | 13 the past

I'm so glad that my sisters are okay and that everyone is well and good, Remi thought to herself as she sat on the beach in Miami.

She had relocated herself after Leigh and she were found from being kidnapped and Demitri was good and dead.

I need peace in my life, she thought. *Where is my Trent to come save me?* She loved Shia, but she envied her to. Shia had a man and a family. Remi was afraid of men. She never knew if she could trust them or not. Even to this day, she hadn't told Shia about the things Demetri had made her do and done to her. She would carry it to her grave. She was embarrassed and ashamed about it all.

I need to come to peace with my life. Remi stared out at the ocean watching as the waves crashed into the shore. The waves are so free. I want to be them. Touching land for a moment then back it to sea I go. Another adventure with new places to see.

Maybe I'll stay out here for the rest of my life. I like being away from that world of deceit though I do miss my heartbeats, my sisters. They complete me.

Digging her toes into the sand, she continued watching the waves come in.

***

"Remi you have to come home," Leigh's anxious voice came across her cell phone.

"Why what's going on?" Remi asked nervous by Leigh's tone.

"Shia's been in an accident. She's in a coma. You have to come back right now," Leigh demanded.

"Oh no." Remi's heart began pounding uncontrollably. "What are the doctor's saying?"

"That as long as she fights for her life, they will fight for it as well," Leigh told her.

"What kind of an accident was she in?"

"A car accident. We can discuss that when you come home. I've already booked your flight. Head to the airport right now," Leigh told her.

136

"Okay, okay. I'll be on my way in a few. How is Trent? I know how much he loves Shia. This must be killing him inside."

"Devastated as you can imagine," Leigh told her. "I swear Remi, how much more can this family go through? We need Shia to be okay for everyone's sake. She's our glue. That's my twin. Nothing bad can happen to her."

"I know Lei Lei. I can't imagine if I had a twin how much more devastating this situation would be."

Leigh sobbed on the phone. "Please get here as soon as you can Rem. I need you."

"I'll be they before you know it."

"Thank you. Please be safe. I can't afford anything to happen to my other sister at the moment."

"I always am. I'll be there soon. I promise."

"Okay. Thank you sis. I love you."

137

***

When Remi arrived at Trent and Shia's home, she had no idea who the woman was that was walking around as if she owned the place.

"So who is this?" Remi asked Leigh, while they played with Joelle in the living room.

"Some straggler named Natalia that Trent used to date that has obviously lost her mind and taken his with her."

"What in the world? I go to Florida for some downtime and come back to chaos in this house. Trent knows better. If Shia were home she would be having none of this."

"That's precisely the message that I have been trying to convey to everyone. But no one seems to be listening to me."

Natalia watched Leigh and Remi through malicious calculating eyes. She could handle the younger sister, but Shia's twin was a whole other problem. The two of them breathing the same air was like a time bomb waiting to ignite.

Leigh and Remi continued playing with Joelle, choosing to ignore Natalia. Especially Leigh, she refused to acknowledge the opportunist woman that was trying, rather successfully it seemed, to take her sisters place.

"Leigh, are you cooking something for the kids or should I order some take out for everyone?" Remi asked.

"You should ask the new Shia that question," Leigh replied, rolling her eyes. "She seems to be campaigning for wifey over there," she told Remi, grateful that her little sister had flown up from Florida to help out the family.

Remi quickly shifted her eyes between the two women. You could slice through the tension in the family room with a butcher knife. Remi watched as Natalia continued to clean up, not paying any attention to Leigh's statements.

"Lei, Lei, what is wrong with you?" Remi chastising Leigh with her eyes, "She's only trying to help for right now. She's not doing anything that I have seen so far. You don't have to be this mean towards her. I want her gone to, but I'm not going to be rude to her. Trent obviously wants her here."

"No Remi, helping is what we are for. She is obviously trying to replace Shia. Remi, please don't be so gullible. She's still the same bitch you asked me about a few moments ago."

A loud boom made both sisters glance in Natalia's direction as she slammed a plate down on the table.

"Do you have something you would like to say to me? I'm standing right here. Be a woman about yours and get it off your chest."

Disdain was apparent in Leigh's demeanor. "I have a lot to say actually." Leigh stood up and left Joelle playing on the floor coming to a stop directly in front of Natalia. Looking her up and down from head to toe.

Remi ran up behind Leigh and grabbed her arm. "Leigh please don't do anything crazy. This wannabe is old news. Trent dated her before our sister, so it's fair to say if he wanted her to really be around he would have made her a part of his life before now."

Leigh ignored Remi and her naïve statements. "You think you're slick, trying to waltz in here and replace my sister, but I can see right through you with your fake good girl manner and your fake Susie homemaker appearance. You're a fraud and I won't stop until I prove it."

"Listen sweetie, trust me when I tell you, you don't want to go toe to toe with a woman like me." Natalia moved in closer to Leigh until their noses were almost touching. "Now be a good little Auntie and play with the children, then carry your happy ass home."

"Oh Shit! No she didn't." Remi quickly stepped in between the two women when she saw Leigh ball her hands into fists.

"This isn't your house, so if anyone is leaving it will be you." Leigh managed to spit out through clinched teeth.

"Trent and I are going to be together, so it will be my house soon enough, mark my words. That being said, I would like for you to leave. You've over stayed your welcome."

"Oh hell no!" Leigh shouted, startling Joelle who began to cry. Remi ran over to the teary toddler to comfort her as Leigh headed to Trent's office to confront him with a smug Natalia close on her heels.

Bursting into Trent's home office without bothering to knock, Leigh was on a ten. Slamming the door behind her in Natalia's face and locking it, she went off on Trent.

"How dare you have this woman walking around this house trying to replace my sister? Shy is in a

COMA, not dead! You better start explaining and you better start now before I begin to think that the two of you tried to kill my sister, so you could be together!" Leigh was clearly hysterical and didn't care.

Trent had glanced up when his office door had been thrown open and rose out of his chair slowly as Leigh ranted and raved in front of him.

"What do you two have going on Trent?" Leigh had tears falling freely from her eyes. "I thought you loved Shia." Leigh shook her head in disbelief. Sadness radiating from every part of her body. "I thought you loved her…"

Trent walked around the office desk and reached for Leigh, attempting to pull her into a hug, but Leigh immediately moved just outside his reach. Trent dropped his arms.

"It's not what you think." He began to explain, "I really do need help with the kids and Natalia has been that. The kids like having her around and it makes my life that much easier."

Leigh shook her head in disbelief. "Remi and I have been here helping you as well. You don't need to do this. Something is up with that crazy chick; I can feel it. Get her out of here." Leigh raised pleading eyes up to his saddened ones. "Please don't do this. Shia would be rolling over in her hospital bed if she knew what was going on in this house."

"I have to do what's best for me and the kids right now. Shia would want me to do what needed to be done to ensure that they would be okay."

"You'll regret this." Leigh said as she began walking toward the office door to unlock it. "I promise you, you will." When she opened the door,

Natalia was standing there with her ever present smile in place.

"Hope you received all the information you needed. Now leave this house now please."

Raising her hand Leigh smacked Natalia as hard as she could removing the smile completely off her face. Leigh hadn't planned to hit her, but there was something about Natalia calling this her house that completely irked Leigh's nerves.

"I'm going to kill you!" Natalia shouted as she punched Leigh in her eye and continued her assault as Leigh grabbed her eye. Trent ran to separate the women immediately picking Natalia up off the floor to get her away from Leigh. Trent held on to a kicking and screaming Natalia allowing Leigh time to get herself together.

"You better watch your step. You're going to get yours. BELIEVE ME ON THAT!" Leigh spat at Natalia as she began to feel her eye swelling. "Trent, I can't believe that you're allowing this piece of trash in here, knowing how classy Shia is. Didn't anyone ever teach you that once you upgrade you never go back down?"

Natalia had finally calmed down in Trent's arms and turned to glare at Leigh.

"You have some nerve," she told Leigh as she pushed her hair behind her ear. "You come in here and attack me and then call me a piece of trash." Natalia laughed long and hard. "The only trash present is you and we don't allow garbage in our rooms. I believe your place is outside. Now please exit my house. Obviously my lessons for teaching you how to be a lady aren't working. If you knew how to take care of home instead of acting like a street urchin, maybe you would have a man. Now get out!"

Leigh narrowed her eyes on Natalia, as she addressed Trent. "As long as she's here," she pointed at Natalia. "I won't be coming back." Leigh quickly ran out the house and into her car leaving Remi behind.

Trent gingerly placed Natalia's feet back on the floor once he heard the front door slam.

"She's never allowed back in this house, is that understood?" Natalia told him.

"Oh hell naw." Remi had finally had enough. "This is my sister's home, you have no right. The only person that needs to leave is your and I'm going to need you to make that step sooner than later."

Natalia stared at Remi. "Like right now." Remi took a

step toward her to show that she was serious and she be taken that way.

Trent quickly stepped in between the two women. "Thanks Remi. I can handle it from here. She'll be leaving." He quickly turned to Natalia, "You should go. Family comes before everything. And you are not family." He informed her as he left her standing in the room.

Remi smirked at the pitiful expression on Natalia's face. "I'll see you out. Take care."

CHAPTER | 14 the present

Nathan awoke to the sound of his phone buzzing. Grabbing it and leaving the room so as not to disturb a sleeping Remi, he answered on his way down the stairs. It was rare that his chief called him personally.

"Hey chief. Everything alright?"

"No everything is not alright," the chief informed him. "There's been a casualty tonight."

Nate's whole body froze. A feeling of dread washing all over his body.

"Please tell me that the boys are okay. Please tell me. I need to hear it."

The hesitation on the other end of the line told me exactly what he needed to know.

"I'm so sorry. They didn't make it."

"What do you mean they didn't make it? What happened to their detail? Why wasn't anyone watching the house or them wherever they were what happened?"

"The detail perished as well," the chief stated matter of factly.

Nathan sat down on the stairs and put his head in his hands.

"This is my fault," he told the chief.

"This isn't your fault Nate. Don't beat yourself up about this. If you had been there, you may be dead as well."

"What am I supposed to tell Remi? I told her that her family was safe. Now I'm supposed to go in there and break the news to her that her nephews are gone. This is going to kill her. She's been through so much."

"I know. The guys over at the scene now trying to figure out what happened. So I have to go. Are you going to be ok?"

Nate was devastated. "Yeah I'll be good. I just have to figure out what I'm going to do or say to Remi. Thanks for letting me know chief."

Nate sat on the steps for a few minutes more. He was in no hurry to go back into the bedroom that he shared with Remi to let her know the news. He decided he would wait until the morning and let her have one last night and peaceful rest.

As soon as Remi woke up the next morning, she knew something was wrong. There was an unsettling feeling in her body. She didn't know what it was but she knew it was something.

"Nate, wake up, something is wrong." She reached to her right side and noticed that he wasn't lying next to her.

"I'm over here." She turned her head at the sound of his voice. He was sitting in the rocking chair that she kept next to the window for when she needed to just look outside and think. His face told her that her feeling was right.

"Why are you sitting over there?"

Nate cleared his throat. "I was watching you sleep."

"Oh. What's wrong?"

Nate stood and approached the bed.

"Your silence is scaring me. Just please tell me," Remi told him. She didn't have time for beating around the bush. She needed to know what was what.

"The twins," Nate began and Remi closed her eyes willing the tears not to fall. "Oh no." She whispered.

"What happened to them?" She began blinking rapidly, trying to keep the tears away. She just knew that she was in for bad news.

Nate pulled her into his arms. "Both were shot in the head. Neither survived."

"What?" Remi's broken sobs began in her stomach and pushed through to her throat and out.

154

"No," she said, shaking her head in between sobs. "Not my babies. This can't be right. This can't be."

Nate stood there holding her stroking her hair. Not sure what to say.

"This shit has got to stop," Remi screamed. "I know Avionne did this. I know she did. I'm sick and tired of her. This is just too much. She's trying to take out our whole family." Remi backed away from Nate's arms. "I can't marry you. I refuse to bring you into this mess with my family. If you become one of us, it puts you in line to die as well. That's our destiny. Save yourself. Our fate is already sealed."

"Don't speak like that. We can figure this out," Nate told her.

"There is nothing to figure out. Go live your life. I am going to live mine. I just have one request; please take Luna and Joelle with you."

155

"What? You no longer want them?" Nate asked her.

"Or course I want them, but I need them to be safe and they're not safe with me. Avionne will come for me next. I just know it and I plan to be ready for her."

Nate grabbed Remi by the shoulders. "You are talking crazy. You cannot take on Avionne alone. She's a maniac."

"Yeah, well so am I. God speed to her because she is going to need it."

Nate shook his head. "This is a bad idea. You can't do this."

"Go live your life Nate. Fall in love with a woman that doesn't have all this drama. I have to let you go."

"I'm not letting you go."

"You don't have a choice in the matter. I'm going to pack up Luna's things and make sure that Joelle is ready as well."

Remi took in the man that she loved, standing in front of her helpless. She should have known better, She'd really thought that she would have an opportunity at happily ever after, but that wasn't in the cards for her. She had to move on. Her family wasn't blessed to have that. Shia had gotten the closest.

"Thank you for showing me what love is and what it can feel like. It's an amazing feeling, but I can no longer live in your fairytale. They aren't real anyway." Remi told Nate. She needed for him to understand that this was indeed over and she was done.

Nate felt himself dying a million deaths. Remi's mind was made up. She was distancing herself away from him and he knew that there was nothing that he could do about it.

CHAPTER | 15 the past

Staring at Krista's slit throat Avionne had little to no remorse.

"I love you Krista, but I could never trust you. If my own mother would leave me to fend for myself, I know that you would do everything the same and I can't have that," Avionne spoke to the corpse.

She was sorry that this had to be Krista's fate but everything must happen for a reason. Kamilah was lucky she wasn't home at the time. Avionne felt as if it might be too obvious if both of them died the same day that she would look like the culprit. At least at this rate she could act as if she walked into a murder herself. Grabbing her things, she decided to take herself to a movie and do what typical eighteen year olds would do.

Returning to the house after her movie she entered at a snail's pace, trying to figure out how to play this scene out. She knew that Kamilah was due to return home at any moment. Making her way to the kitchen she flicked the light switch on and nothing happened. Loving the plan that she had created, she was elated to see everything working out. She'd cut the electricity line before she'd reentered the house.

Doing her best to make it appear as if someone had just ran on a killing spree in the house, but the only one there was Krista so they decided to make it as gruesome as possible, Avionne knew that she had a winner. Pulling her hand away from the switch, she basked in the wetness that she felt on her hand. This way it would look as if she had been trying to see and would explain why her DNA was all over the place in the crime scene.

Avionne's head and heart began to pound simultaneously. All of a sudden, she was having a hard time breathing. The air in her lungs was quickly running out and she felt as if she were suffocating in he own skin. This was a hard kill for her. She'd loved Krista. She prayed that she wasn't having a heart attack. It would not do her well to die on her birthday.

161

Hearing the front door slam, Avionne quickly pressed herself flat against the wall. She wanted it to look as if she was frightened for her life.

"Avi, you in here?"

Avionne sighed a breath of relief when she heard her foster sister Kamilah's voice yelling out to her.

"Yeah, I'm here," Avionne yelled back, while exiting the kitchen.

"Something is up with our electricity. I called the electric company and they should be fixing the problem soon."

"Good," Avionne said as she walked up to Kamilah to give her a hug. "I was worried; I thought something had happened to you."

Kamilah let out a laugh, "Why? Because the lights are off? Avi, you have to lighten up. You've been so uptight lately."

"I know," Avionne said, releasing Kamilah. "I really have got to learn how to relax."

"Hey, have you seen Tiki? I've been calling out to her, but she won't stop hiding."

Avionne hated Tiki. Unfortunately, Tiki had managed to survive the slaying because he had run away and she hadn't had time to find him. Tiki was Kamilah's cat. She had gotten Tiki when she was twelve as a gift from her biological Dad who had passed away.

"Uh Kami, maybe you should sit down." Avionne began.

"What's wrong?" Kamilah enveloped Avionne into another hug. "What is going on? It's your birthday you can't be so down like this."

Avionne opened her mouth to speak, but before a word could come out, the lights flickered back on.

Now that is a surprise. Avionne was genuinely shocked. *How did the lights come back on?* She wondered

"Lights!" Kamilah exclaimed as she released Avionne and turned to survey the room. "Great. Tiki! Where are you?" Kamilah turned back to face Avionne, "It's not like her to be this quiet. You think she's hiding or something. Maybe she's in the kitchen eating?" she said as she headed for the kitchen doorway.

Avionne stayed where she was allowing Kamilah to wander around the house without her.

Everyone in the neighborhood could hear Kamilah's blood curling scream, Avionne was sure of it. Staying rooted to the spot that she was in she watched as Kamilah came running out the kitchen with a haunted look on her face with Tiki in her arms.

164

"It's, it's a," Kamilah was stuttering so bad that Avionne had no choice but to play her part and look in the kitchen to see what was going on. Walking apprehensively into the kitchen she stopped short. There, hanging from their ceiling, was their foster mother Krista. Avionne could see that her neck was broken as it hung on the rope. Feeling her heart leap into her throat, Avionne stared at the body hanging from the ceiling, wondering if Krista would figure out that she was the culprit. Krista had been her mother for the past seven years. The best mother anyone could ever ask for and now she was gone, which meant Avionne had no one now. Now she would be free to find her biological mother. It was time.

Leaving the kitchen, Avionne walked past Kamilah without saying a word and went to her room. Throwing some of her clothes and other belongings into a bag, she wanted to put as much distance as possible between she and her foster mother's body that was hanging in the kitchen. She knew that there was no way that she could stay around this chaos. Walking back into the living room, she saw Kamilah hunched on the sofa with Tiki crying. Without so much as a goodbye, Avionne left. It's not that she didn't love Krista and Kamilah, because she did, but no one knew the true story about her background and her biological mother. If she stayed in that house with that body hanging like that, someone was sure to do their research and try to blame it all on her eventually and she couldn't have that. She couldn't have that at all.

CHAPTER 16 the present

"Mommy can I have a cookie?" Lucas was standing in Avionne's face with a hopeful expression on his face.

"It's *may I* and the answer is no." Avionne told him. "It's almost your dinner time."

"You're being mean Mommy."

"I'll be that. Now go cleanup for dinner."

"Yes ma'am."

"We have him trained so well."

Avionne snorted, "We huh?"

"Yes *we*. I've been helping you raise him all this time," Payton pointed out.

Avionne sighed slightly annoyed. Payton seemed to work her nerves every day now. She chose to keep quiet and not say anything.

Enough was enough. She was still reeling from her high of shooting the twins. *I've missed killing*, she thought to herself. *I've taken too much of a break, it's time to get back to doing my thing.*

"I've decided that I want to go back and do my own thing now." Payton suddenly announced.

"Oh really?" Avionne gave her full undivided attention to Payton. "And what exactly does that mean?"

"It means," Payton stopped for emphasis. "I no longer wish to live this lifestyle. I prefer to do my own thing with my own life and I wish you and Lucas nothing but the best."

Avionne was taken aback. "So I leave you to your own defenses to come up with what you want to do and this is what you come back to me with?" she tells Payton staring at her as if she were a fire breathing dragon with two heads. *Stupid girl.* "Well if that's your decision I respect it."

"Really?"Payton asked visibly shocked. "So you're just going to let me walk away?"

"Payton, you're not a hostage. You are free to go whenever you like." Avionne politely told her.

"Well actually I was thinking since the house is in my name that you and Lucas could start looking

169

for somewhere else to stay."

Avionne began to laugh hysterically. "Oh so you're putting me and Lucas out on the street?" *The audacity of this girl. She had no value over her life whatsoever.*

Payton was shocked and appalled that she would think that. "I would never do anything like that. You and Lucas are more than welcome to stay until you find somewhere to go. I'm not going to make you homeless."

Avionne stood up to stir the pasta that she had on the stove cooking up for Lucas. Without a second thought, she flung the hot pasta and pan at Payton's head.

"Bitch are you fucking crazy," Avionne yelled as Payton bent in the fetal position to try and defend herself against the attack.

Picking up the pan, Avionne continued to beat Payton over the head with it. "Now look at your dumb ass. Bet you don't think you all high and mighty now." She continued screaming.

"Mommy what are you doing?" a small voice asked from the doorway.

At the sound of Lucas voice, Avionne dropped the bloodied pan to the floor.

"Hey baby, I didn't know you were standing there." Avionne was feeling like a thief caught in the act.

"What did you do to Auntie Payton?" Lucas cried

Avionne rushed over to him and grabbed his face. "Auntie Payton was being a bad girl so she got punished. You make sure you're always a good boy so you don't have to be punished like that, okay."

Lucas nodded.

"Good boy. Now go to your room while I prepare you some dinner and clean up this mess."

"Okay Mommy."

Avionne watched him leave the kitchen to go to his room and then returned her attention to Payton.

Smiling as she watched her struggle to breath. The right side of her skull caved in. *I live for this.*

Removing her cast iron skillet from the cabinet, she bent over Payton's body.

"I appreciate all that you have done for Lucas and me. We will never forget you, but I have to let you go on to the other side now because you have lost your damn mind. Thinking you're going to put my child and I out. See that's where you went all wrong. I would have let you leave and come after you later in life. At the very least, you wouldn't be lying on the floor bleeding to death struggling for air to breath.

172

But disloyalty must be punished." Avionne gazed into Payton's eyes with a smirk on her face. "I love you honey. May you rest in peace," she told her, as she brought the heavy skillet down on Payton's head watching her skull collapse beneath the force. *Damn that felt good.* She thought as she picked up the skillet and the pan taking them to the sink to wash them off.

Picking up the phone out the cradle Avionne auto dialed the pizza parlor and ordered her and Lucas a pizza for dinner. Payton had worn her out. She was no longer in the mood to fix Lucas a homemade dinner.

Walking upstairs to the closet, she grabbed her handsaw. It was time to cut up the food for the neighborhood animals. They were going to have a good day in the morning.

Avionne smiled, she was all about being a Good

Samaritan.

CHAPTER 17 the past

"Leigh, Joelle is missing," Remi told Leigh as soon as she entered the house.

"What do you mean she is missing?" Leigh looked at Remi sideways. "She likes to play hide and seek. She may just be hiding somewhere waiting for you to find her. I mean have you looked?"

Remi was offended. "Oh course I looked. What kind of question is that? Listen to me, I already thought of her playing hide and seek. The girl is missing."

Leigh shook her head as she began calling Joelle's name throughout the house with Remi close on her heels. "How in the hell did you manage to lose her? What where you doing?" Leigh turned her accusing eyes on Remi.

Remi couldn't believe that Leigh was speaking to her this way. As if she would knowingly put their niece's life in danger in any form or fashion. "I put her down for a nap. And began cleaning the house," Remi told her as she burst into tears. "I didn't mean for this to happen."

"Rem cut the shit okay. No tears, you hear me. We don't have time for this with everything going on with Shia too. We just need to find Joelle and find her quickly before Trent gets back from the hospital.

"What's going on?" he shouted through the house. "Remi! Where are you?" Remi ran into the foyer with a frantic Leigh right behind her.

Seeing Leigh made Trent want to panic, but he fought to keep his composure. "What is going on?" he asked again more calmly.

"Joelle is hiding somewhere." Remi responded.

"Is that all?" Trent instantly relaxed. "You two almost made me lose my mind. How long has she been hiding?"

"Two hours." Remi cringed.

Trent wasn't in the mood for this right now. He needed peace. He prayed his wife came out of her coma soon.

"Joelle, that's enough playtime. Come out right now." Trent yelled in a stern tone expecting Joelle to pop up out of wherever she was hiding.

"Trent we've tried that and checked everywhere. She's not here."

"What do you mean not here?" Trent turned angry eyes on her. "If she's not here, where else would she be?" Redirecting his wrath toward Remi. "I leave my daughter in your care for a couple of hours and you lose her. Where could she have gone?"

Remi hung her head down. "I'm sorry. I don't know where she is." Trent was also accusing her of doing something to his daughter. She couldn't understand what was up with him and Leigh. She would never intentionally hurt her niece.

Trent went to his bedroom and checked under the bed. He had to find his baby girl. She was all he had of him and Shia. He couldn't live with himself if something happened to Joelle.

He tried to think like a toddler to figure out where she had wondered too, when the doorbell rang.

Trent raced to the front door throwing it open.

There stood Natalia with a sleeping Joelle cradled in her arms. Trent closed his eyes in relief. His baby girl had been found.

Graciously taking Joelle out of Natalia's arms, Trent didn't know whether to hug her or call the police for kidnapping.

"I was coming over to talk to you about the other night and saw this little one lying in the grass fast asleep."

"Thanks for being here Natalia. I don't know how she got out the house."

"Me either," Leigh said accusingly staring at Natalia through suspicious eyes. "Seems a little convenient to me. Don't you think so Remi?"

"Yeah, crazy how Joelle suddenly disappears and out of nowhere reappears with Natalia who shows up out of nowhere unannounced. Seems very convenient to me as well, especially since we searched high and low for her." Remi said eyeing Natalia as well. *This lying bitch.*

"Doesn't matter," Trent said breaking the tension, "I'm just glad Joelle is back safely. "Come on in Natalia. You said you wanted to talk."

Trent led Natalia to the family room and sat on the chaise lying Joelle across his lap as to not disturb her sleep.

"What's up?" Trent asked.

Natalia shrugged, "I want to apologize about the other day. I was very inappropriate and out of line. Please forgive me."

"You found my little girl. I'd forgive you anything."

Natalia gazed at him in appreciation.

Remi and Leigh observed Trent and Natalia's interaction from the hallway.

"I don't trust this heiffa. Something is up with her," Leigh whispered to Remi.

"I know. I don't trust her either, but I don't know what we can do about the situation. I can't stay here forever. I have to get back to Florida in a couple days.

Leigh understood that Remi had to get back to her life; she'd already been up here with them for weeks hoping that Shia would wake out of her coma.

Leigh sighed, "I know you have to leave soon. We are just going to have to figure something out."

***

Remi thought Shia looked so peaceful lying in her hospital bed. It almost appeared as if she were merely asleep and not in a coma.

"She doesn't even look as if she's been in an accident anymore."

"I know," Leigh replied to Remi's statement. The nurse's had removed all of Shia's casts. The only thing left was her head wrap and the nurses had said that would be coming off soon also. "She looks good. Almost brand new."

"I miss her."

"I know you do, but Shia will fight through and be stronger than ever. "You'll see," Leigh reassured Remi.

r it," Remi replied leaning

na on the forehead. "I love you Shy,

okay. We want you to pull out of this so

you can come on home," Remi whispered

ering over her.

She needed her big sister, she was the only

mother that she had left.

CHAPTER | 18 the present

Remi was now in full-fledge get back mode. Avionne had made her life a living hell. She'd had to give up her man, both of her sisters were dead, her nephews were dead, her parents were dead. See had no one left. All because of Phylicia. This stemmed from her down to her daughter. Both were two apples off the same exact rotten tree and Kelt

had had enough. No more running. She began to

understand Trent's mentality before he died. There

was no way someone could hide or run forever.

Eventually at some point, you had to face what was

happening right in front of you. That was the only

way to go about the whole thing.

I see now that this is my fate. I won't see old age.

I won't have children of my own. I'm meant to take

down Avionne. That is my sole purpose in life. I

understand now. I get it. I had a few great years to see

what being a mother is like and I'll always be grateful

to God for giving me the opportunity even though the

circumstances that brought about the situation were

dire.

This is it for me, Remi thought as she sat at the computer surfing the internet for ways to commit murder in the most grotesque way imaginable.

It's time for Avionne to get a dose of her own medicine running around terrifying people. Like mother, like daughter.

Her ringing cell took her out of her hate-filled daze. Seeing Nate's number, she answered immediately.

"Hi Nate." She gushed. How are the girls?"

"The girls are doing great. Missing their auntie a lot though."

"Yeah? Even Joelle's little evil ass?" Remi laughed.

"Yes. Even Joelle. She's being a model citizen over here."

"Mmhmmn I bet she is. That's because you don't play."

Nate laughed, "In other news we have a photo of the person that murdered your nephews. You won't believe who it is."

"It's Avionne isn't it? I just know it is."

"Well actually, the lady in the video looks exactly like Shia."

Remi froze. "Come again?"

"You heard me right. When I saw the surveillance that got me thinking to that day that you had gone to the grocery store and ran into a woman that looked exactly like your sister with the same name. I have a theory that Avionne had her face reconstructed to look exactly like Shia to throw you and the kids off your game. Seems as if she went all the way in by changing her face and then her name to Shia as well."

"That sick bitch!" Remi spat out. "I knew something was up with her that day she appeared out of nowhere. Everything was too circumstantial. I mean what are the odds of that happening to anyone?"

"She must have played on that when she went to see the boys, that's why they let her in. They were confused. All of you are missing Shia so it's expected that your heart wants to believe what is right in front of your face even though your head knows better."

"My poor nephews. They never stood a chance. They missed their mama so much. I mean we all did."

"Yeah, so that's just a heads up. Be on the lookout for her now that you know what's what."

"I will definitely be doing that. Thank you so much for helping me. You know I will always love you, right?"

"You know you don't have to go this route right'? Nate asked her. "Let me protect you."

"I wish I could honey, but this is something I must go at alone. Thank you for being the man I wanted to spend the rest of my life with. You will remain in my heart forever. Just take very good care of my girls. They mean the world to me. Good-bye."

There was nothing Nate could do. He knew that she meant it. This is where their road divided. She was going her way and he was going his. "Goodbye my love. I'll never forget you."

Remi hung up the phone with Nate without a tear falling. She had already said her goodbyes in her heart. It was time for her to let him go so that he could move on. He deserved that. A woman with no drama. A life that he could be happy in without worrying about her every day of his life.

CHAPTER 19 the past

"Congratulations! You have a son," the doctor announced. Avionne heard the doctor but was too weak to speak at the moment. Still on the operating table where she'd had to have an emergency C-section because the baby's heartbeat was dropping she was ecstatic by the news.

Her eyes had the audacity to mist up on her. She was someone's mother. She couldn't believe it.

"God, I know I am not your favorite person in the world, but I thank you so much for sparing my son's life. She'd never been so happy to hear a baby crying at the top of their lungs in all her life.

"How is she doing?" She heard Harris ask the doctor.

"She's going to be alright. Lost a lot of blood, but we're going to take good care of her."

"When can she hold him?"

"When we get her all settled. Won't be too much longer now," the doctor told him.

Avionne was happy by that news. She couldn't wait to get her son into her arms.

"Great news," Harris responded.

"Knock, knock, you have visitors," a nurse announced from the doorway.

Avionne looked away from her son smiling. Her smile slipped away once she saw the officers at her door, her heart sinking. *They've finally caught up to me.*

"Hello miss. You are being placed under arrest." The officers told her.

Avionne wanted to bolt off of the table, but knew that there was no way that she could. She couldn't even feel her legs yet from the surgery.

"You have the right to remain silent. Anything you say can and will be used against you in a court of law. You have the right to an attorney. If you cannot afford an attorney, one will be provided for you. Do you understand the rights I have just read to you?"

Avionne nodded.

"With these rights in mind, do you wish to speak to me?" the officer asked Avionne.

"No, I do not choose to speak with you." Avionne glanced over at Harris. "What is happening? Did you know anything about this?" She snapped at him. "I just had my baby. The doctor won't allow it."

"Why are you asking me about your situation?" he asked her with a grin. "I'm not the one arresting you."

Avionne narrowed her eyes as she took in Harris' grinning face. *So you want to play hardball,* she thought.

"How can I be under arrest? I've done nothing wrong," she politely told the officers, choosing to ignore Harris.

"Do you know someone by the name Kamilah Wright, ma'am?"

That little shit. She frowned up her face. "I have an adopted sister by that name," she told them.

"You killed her. They have the body. It's over Avionne," Harris told her pointblank, sick of playing games with her.

Oh, you're damn right it is. Your life will be over. She glared at Harris. "I have no idea what you're talking about."

"That's fine, you don't have to. These nice boys are going to wait with you until the doctor allows you to leave and then they will take you away anyway." Harris winked at her. "They're hoping that they will be able to jog your memory."

Focusing narrowed eyes on Harris, Avionne wished with everything in her that she could get off the table and slit his throat.

"Ma'am, please stand."

"I've just had surgery," Avionne's anguished reply resonated off the walls. "I can't stand. You can't do this. What about my son?"

"He's my son too. We'll be fine without you." Harris interrupted.

"You will not get away with this." Avionne snapped at him.

Harris continued smiling. Avionne was beside herself in anger. She hoped Harris enjoyed his time with their son, because as of today, his days on earth were numbered.

CHAPTER | 20 the present | The Finale

Remi watched Avionne from a distance. This had been her daily routine for over the past month. She made it a point to know every place that Avionne visited. If she walked down the street, if she got something to eat, if she took a walk, if she took a shit Remi knew exactly what was going on at all times.

She had had enough of Avionne and her mess. The hunter had finally become the hunted.

Remi watched her with her son every day. By normal standards, she had to hand it to Avionne; she seemed like a good mother. Always watching her son, holding his hand the few times she brought him out the house when he crossed the street, playing with him in the house. When Avionne was with him, she seemed like your average day to day person.

But Remi was no fool. Avionne was anything but average. Anyone who changes their appearance to look like someone other than themselves for the sole purpose of bringing harm to that family is certifiable.

Smiling because her spirit was finally at peace, Remi knew what she needed to do. She was okay with her decision, the next steps that she would take and more than ready to welcome the unknown. This was the only way for her to insure that her family was safe. Tonight was the night.

Pulling her cell phone out of her denim jacket pocket, she dialed Nate's number wanting to hear the deep sultry sound of his voice.

"Hello beautiful. To what do I owe the pleasure?"

She sighed in appreciation. The smooth velvet of his voice caressed Remi's psyche.

"I just needed to hear you breathe. You feel so near me tonight," Remi told him.

Nate's heart sank to the floor. He knew what this was, she was saying goodbye.

"I can't change your mind huh?" He asked softly, voice barely above a whisper.

Remi knew him well enough to know that he was fighting the urge to cry.

"No." She whispered back. "I have to protect what's left of my family. Those two girls deserve a chance and I'm going to see to it that they have one come hell or high water."

Nate cleared his voice, "They miss you."

"I know. I miss them too. Please let them know that everything I do is for their benefit. They will live a long prosperous life because I won't and for that reason alone I can leave here knowing they will be okay."

"What about me?"

"Oh Nate, I wish that I could stay for you, but I can't." Remi paused to get her emotions in check before continuing, "You will find a beautiful woman to love that will love you back. You will get married and hopefully have kids of your own one day. I want that for you. You promise me." Remi urged him.

Nate's dam of tears finally descended down his face. "I don't know if that is something that I can promise."

"Please Nate, promise me. I need to hear that from you. I need to hear it." She begged.

"I promise," came Nathan's tortured response.

"Thank you." Remi shut her eyes. "Thank you."

"Do you want to speak with the girls?"

"No, that will be much too hard for me and for them. Please just tell them I love them. I love you too."

"And I you."

"I know you do. I'm glad to have gotten the opportunity to meet you. You changed everything for me.

Remi hung up the phone as soon as the words left her mouth. If she stayed on the phone with him any longer, she was going too lose her nerve and that was something that she couldn't afford to do.

This was her moment. Glancing around once more to make sure no one was outside; she calmly retreated from the car.

It's now or never, she thought to herself. *I have to do what I have to do. Forward march honey, forward March.*

***

Avionne watched her from the house. She'd been wondering when Remi was going to make her move. The last month had been pure comedy to Avionne. She was a professional at the game Remi thought she wanted to play. Avionne had known the very first day that Remi had decided to follow her and she had let her. This was the most excitement she'd felt in a long time. There was nothing like a game of cat and mouse, especially when the mouse thought that she was the cat.

This is going to be a great night. Avionne smiled to herself as she watched Remi's attempt to blend into the shadows of the night. A great night indeed. The games were beginning. *I just love festivities.*

***

Remi was anxious; she wanted nothing more than to get this whole ordeal over with. No more delaying. The sooner the better. I'm ready, she thought.

Walking up to the side of the house, Remi was surprised to see a window open. *That seems strange*, she thought to herself. There had never been a window open before especially on such a chilly night.

Choosing to bypass the window, Remi stuck to her original plan, until her plan was taken away from her.

The back door opened suddenly and a smiling Avionne stepped out of the door.

"I'm so glad you came to visit Remi. Won't you come in." Eyes sparkling, Avionne looked radiant.

Remi was in shock. "How did you know I was here?"

"Oh fiddle faddle. It's all nonsense. I've been expecting you for awhile now. I'm so glad you chose tonight to drop in." Avionne waved her hand past her face. "This is where we are now. Shall we?" Avionne asked Remi as she extended her hand for her to take.

Remi stared her nemesis in the eye. "Yes, I believe we shall."

"Oh goodie," Avionne squealed. I have such an amazing evening for us planned.

203

Remi walked into the house instantly drawing her gun and pointed it at the back of Avionne's head, cocking the trigger not remotely interested in what Avionne thought she had up her sleeve.

Avionne whirled around at the sound. "Oh fooey." She stated looking disappointed. "I see you want to get the festivities started sooner than later and right before the appetizer," she sighed. "Well so be it."

Remi didn't wait for her to move she pulled the trigger and the first shot rang out hitting Avionne in the right shoulder.

Avionne staggered back from the curve of the shot in shock. She'd never expected Remi to shoot her. Never in a million years had the thought crossed her mind. She honestly hadn't thought the girl had it in her.

Swiftly pulling a knife out her pocket with her left hand, she threw it with all her might, a grin spread across her face when it hit her target deep in the temple.

The screaming that came with it was what Avionne enjoyed the most. She loved hearing others in pain.

"Did you honestly think that you were just going to come over here and shoot me and that would be the end of it? I'm better at this game than you are Remi. Let it go. I can handle a flesh wound in my shoulder you're going to die from my knife to your neck. Was it really worth it?" Avionne shouted at her in glee.

Remi couldn't deny that she was in agony, but she was not leaving this earth before she did what she came to do, mustering all the strength that was in her she aimed the gun towards Avionne's head and pulled the trigger. The force knocked her off balance and she fell to the floor. She was losing blood quickly. *Shia and Leigh I'm coming to join you. The sisters will be united once again. I love you guys. I'm coming.*

Avionne saw a piece of her brain fall to the floor before she began to lose consciousness. *You live by the sword you die by the sword. I deserve this,* she thought as she slumped to the floor ready to meet her maker.

To join our mailing list for new release updates and free giveaways TEXT GOOD2GO to 42828.

Email mycheawrites@yahoo.com

www.mychea.com

Books by Good2Go Authors on Our Bookshelf

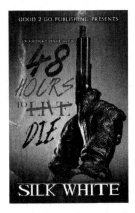

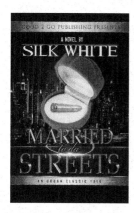

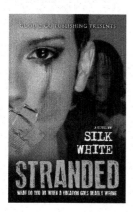

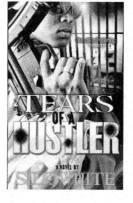

GOOD 2 GO PUBLISHING PRESENTS
A NOVEL BY
SILKWHITE

TEARS OF A HUS3LER

A NOVEL BY
SILK WHITE

GOOD 2 GO PUBLISHING PRESENTS
SILK WHITE

TEARS OF A HUS4LER
YOU'VE BEEN WARNED

A NOVEL BY
SILK WHITE

A NOVEL BY
SILKWHITE

TEARS OF A HUS5LER
THE SPADES

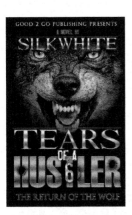

GOOD 2 GO PUBLISHING PRESENTS
A NOVEL BY
SILKWHITE

TEARS OF A HUS6LER
THE RETURN OF THE WOLF

THE TEFLON QUEEN
A NOVEL BY
SILK WHITE

THE TEFLON QUEEN 2
A NOVEL BY
SILK WHITE

THE TEFLON QUEEN 3
HARD TO KILL
SILK WHITE

THE TEFLON QUEEN 4
MR. DEATH
SILK WHITE

GOOD 2 GO PUBLISHING PRESENTS
THE PANTY RIPPER
A NOVEL BY
REALITY WAY

Good 2 Go Films Presents

THE HAND I WAS DEALT- FREE WEB SERIES

NOW AVAILABLE ON YOUTUBE!

YOUTUBE.COM/SILKWHITE212

To order books, please fill out the order form below:

To order films please go to www.good2gofilms.com

Name:_____

Address:_____

City: _____ State: _____ Zip Code: _____

Phone:_____

Email:_____

Method of Payment: Check   VISA   MASTERCARD

Credit Card#:_____

Name as it appears on card: _____

Signature: _____

Item Name	Price	Qty	Amount
48 Hours to Die – Silk White	$14.99		
Business Is Business – Silk White	$14.99		
Business Is Business 2 – Silk White	$14.99		
Flipping Numbers – Ernest Morris	$14.99		
Flipping Numbers 2 – Ernest Morris	$14.99		
He Loves Me, He Loves You Not - Mychea	$14.99		
He Loves Me, He Loves You Not 2 - Mychea	$14.99		
He Loves Me, He Loves You Not 3 - Mychea	$14.99		
He Loves Me, He Loves You Not 4 – Mychea	$14.99		
He Loves Me, He Loves You Not 5 – Mychea	$14.99		
Married To Da Streets – Silk White	$14.99		
My Besties – Asia Hill	$14.99		
My Boyfriend's Wife - Mychea	$14.99		
Never Be The Same – Silk White	$14.99		
Stranded – Silk White	$14.99		
Slumped – Jason Brent	$14.99		
Tears of a Hustler - Silk White	$14.99		
Tears of a Hustler 2 - Silk White	$14.99		
Tears of a Hustler 3 - Silk White	$14.99		
Tears of a Hustler 4- Silk White	$14.99		
Tears of a Hustler 5 – Silk White	$14.99		
Tears of a Hustler 6 – Silk White	$14.99		
The Panty Ripper - Reality Way	$14.99		
The Panty Ripper 3 – Reality Way	$14.99		
The Teflon Queen – Silk White	$14.99		
The Teflon Queen 2 – Silk White	$14.99		

The Teflon Queen 3 – Silk White	$14.99		
The Teflon Queen 4 – Silk White	$14.99		
Time Is Money - Silk White	$14.99		
Young Goonz – Reality Way	$14.99		
Subtotal:			
Tax:			
Shipping (Free) U.S. Media Mail:			
Total:			

Make Checks Payable To:
Good2Go Publishing
7311 W Glass Lane,
Laveen, AZ 85339

12\15

CPSIA information can be obtained
at www.ICGtesting.com
Printed in the USA
LVOW01s1557191115
463343LV00014B/851/P